A Texas Jubilee

Jim Lee, ca. 1951, Japan

Stories from the Lone Star State

James Ward Lee

With a Foreword by Jeff Guinn

Library of Congress Cataloging-in-Publication Data

Lee, James Ward, 1931-
A Texas jubilee : stories from the Lone Star State / James Ward Lee.
p. cm.
Summary: "A Texas Jubilee is a collection of short stories about life in fictional Bodark Springs, Texas. Through these stories, author Jim Lee paints a humorous picture of the politics, friendships, and secrets that are part of day-to-day life in this eccentric little Texas town."--Barnes & Noble website.
ISBN 978-0-87565-513-0 (alk. paper)
1. Christmas--Texas--Fiction. 2. Small cities--Texas--Fiction. 3. Texas--Social life and customs--Fiction. I. Title.
PS3612.E2238T49 2012
813'.6--dc23

2012038997

TCU Press
P.O. Box 298300
Fort Worth, Texas 76129
817.257.7822
www.prs.tcu.edu

To order books: 1.800.826.8911

Designed by Barbara Mathews Whitehead

To Diane, Gyde, Joyce, Ruth, and Sharon

And to Wayne Ray

They stood by me.

The past is a foreign country:
they do things differently there.
—L. P. Hartley

Contents

Foreword

Most readers think it's easier to write short stories than a full-length novel, and that's as wrong as a thought can get. Those of us who write for a living know it's damned near impossible to craft memorable scenes and characters in such a limited number of pages, let alone do it well and often enough to have the makings of a short-story collection. The collections that do reach print almost invariably disappoint, with maybe one or two good stories and the rest of them forgettable dreck. This makes James Ward Lee's *A Texas Jubilee* doubly special; here is an author who not only conjures exceptional reading in short, lyrical bursts, but pulls it off time after glorious time. These thirteen tales of the small Northeast Texas town of Bodark Springs in the 1930s and '40s are as good as anything in years. In recent memory, perhaps only Robert Olen Butler's *Had A Good Time* and Pam Houston's *Cowboys Are My Weakness* match up in terms of pulling us in on the first page and breaking our hearts on the last one because there aren't any more gem-like tales left. The best storytellers always leave us satisfied and yet wanting more, and that's what Jim Lee accomplishes here.

And that may surprise some people. Jim's been a standout in Texas literary circles for decades, as a teacher and an editor and a critic and an essayist. His credentials include membership in both the Texas Institute of Letters and the Texas Literary

Hall of Fame. But the scoundrel's been holding out on us all that time—he can also create the kind of fiction that makes you laugh out loud or breaks your heart and sometimes does both at the same time.

Even if you aren't of a certain age, and even if you haven't been to that part of the Northeast Texas-Oklahoma border where Ernest Tubb is a more respected philosopher than Plato What's-His-Name, you still know *A Texas Jubilee's* memorable cast of characters. Most of the featured ones are from the Dell family, county postman Grady and his much younger wife Mamie and their kids Jackie and Tommy Earl, plus Granny, who was a child back in the Civil War, and nephew J. T. and his wife Hattie, both three-hundred pounders. Grady drinks and Mamie sneaks off some afternoons with John Houston to the Rose Hills Tourist Cabins where it's so romantic, and everybody interacts with other Eastis County denizens who are at once familiar and uniquely memorable. Just consider Edna Earle Morris, the town sex symbol, who claims that one day Jesus dropped in to visit while she was doing her ironing, and he was tall and blond just like Wayne Morris in the 1937 film *Kid Galahad*. Or, perhaps, my personal favorite, ten-year-old Peavine Deerfield, who tries to get himself baptized at every revival meeting, missing out only on sanctification by Mormons, Episcopalians, Catholics, and Unitarians because "there were none of them in Bodark." How about St. Louis Cardinals' pitcher Harry "Foots" Waller, the town's most famous citizen, who gets out of World War II army duty thanks to his flat, size-sixteen feet only to be coerced into serving as Bodark's head air-raid warden, tasked with spotting any waves of German or Japanese bombers trying to use the town's lights at night to find their way to Fort Worth? I promise you that there is literary richness on every page.

Jim builds these stories out of equal parts imagination, history, and heart. *A Texas Jubilee* captures the quirky past without mocking it and reminds us that, for all the changes in the world since, human nature has remained essentially the same. Only the finest writers can make that case without getting cloying or preachy. After reading this collection, you'll have all the proof you need that James Ward Lee ranks among them.

Jeff Guinn
Fort Worth, Texas

Acknowledgments

I wish to thank the editors of the following publications where these stories first appeared, often in very different versions.

Concho River Review (edited by Terence Dalrymple) for "The Return of Jesse James."

Texas Short Stories (edited by Billy Bob Hill) for "Rock-Ola."

Texas Short Fiction (edited by Billy Bob Hill) for "The Pink Petticoat."

Texas Short Stories II (edited by Billy Bob Hill and Laurie Champion) for "It's The Law."

This Place of Memory (edited by Joyce Gibson Roach) for "Four Roses Whiskey," originally titled "Tubby's Trailer."

Southwestern American Literature (edited by Mark Busby) for "Navy Blue and Gold."

A Texas Christmas (edited by John Edward Weems) for "Xmas Tree, O Xmas Tree."

No book succeeds without many hands. I owe a great deal to Dan Williams, director of TCU Press, who encouraged me to get these stories together. To Kathy Walton, who edited these stories with intelligence, wit, and a gentle pen. To Jeff Guinn, whose introduction is more than generous. To Melinda Esco, a genius production manager. To Ruth McAdams, who read these stories and offered valuable criticism.

To Judy Alter and Susan Petty Moneyhon, late of TCU Press, for encouragement. To Terence Dalrymple and Billy Bob Hill, two extraordinary editors. To Raymond Carver for adapting "It's the Law" for readers' theatre. Finally, to the dead—my parents, friends, and relatives—who lived these stories in an almost forgotten past. That past was indeed a foreign country, and we *did* do things differently there.

ONE

Xmas Tree, O Xmas Tree

1928

Grady Dell hated Christmas.

And he hated Homer Brantley.

At least he hated Homer around Christmastime because Homer ordered a lot of packages parcel post that filled up the back seat of Grady's old 490 Chevrolet. He couldn't leave the packages at the mailbox. He had to walk what seemed like a mile up a muddy drive to put them on the porch if Homer wasn't home.

This Christmas Eve Homer not only had three packages, but, what was worse, Homer had a registered letter. That meant that Grady had to stop his car, get out, and track Homer down to sign for the letter.

There was never any telling where Homer was rambling around on any given day. Homer, who had lost an arm in the war, had what Grady thought was a cushy job as caretaker for the Bodark Springs Waterworks out on Eastis County Lake, and Homer was always off somewhere looking at the dam or using his good arm to skim rocks across the lake.

"Sometimes I hate that one-armed son of a bitch," Grady mumbled to himself.

"Christmas gift!" Homer hollered from behind Grady's car.

"Goddamn, Homer, you scared me out of a year's growth," Grady said, "slipping up on me like that and screaming in my ear."

Then Grady relented and said, "Christmas gift yourself. I am glad you showed up. I got all these damned packages and a registered letter that you have got to sign for. Who the hell would send you a registered letter anyway? And on Christmas Eve."

"I bet it's from old Sam Rayburn up in Congress."

"Naw, hell, it ain't from Congress. That would be on the return. This is smeared but it says something about the war department."

"I guess they are telling me one more time how sorry they are that I lost an arm in the Argonne Forest. They may be sorry, but they don't never send no money. That was one sorry battle for me, but you was in the Argonne, so you know how shitty that whole deal was."

"Yeah," Grady said, "we went into that massacre led by a colonel and came out led by a corporal." Grady always said mass-a-cree like the old folks who had been out West in the Indian Wars said it. And he always brought up the fact that they lost so many men and had to come out with nobody higher than a corporal. Grady had been a PFC and figured if it had been much worse, he might have been leading the 18th infantry regiment out of the forest himself.

Grady was over hating Homer and would be till Homer ordered a bunch of heavy parcel-post packages next year. Grady remembered how Homer was usually near the mailbox when Grady brought the mail. He lived alone and was about as desperate for company as anybody on Grady's rural route, which covered part of Eastis County and part of Fannin. Grady had been delivering mail out of Bodark Springs Post Office since he got out of the army in 1919. Besides that, he had been born and raised on the edge of Eastis and Fannin and knew nearly everybody in both counties.

"You got your tree up yet?" Homer asked Grady.

"Not yet."

"How come? It's already Christmas Eve."

Grady laughed. "You don't have to tell me it's Christmas Eve. The only time worse for a mail carrier is when the Sears and Roebuck catalogs come out. But tomorrow'll end the worst of the Christmas rush."

"You government men are about the only people I know who have to work on Christmas Day. You ought to write old Sam a letter about it," Homer said.

"Which Sam? Uncle Sam or Sam Rayburn?" Grady asked.

"I guess either one of 'em. It'd do about the same good, wouldn't it?" Homer laughed.

"Yeah, I reckon so," Grady said. "No good at all. If Calvin Coolidge wants it hauled on Christmas Day, it'll get hauled on Christmas Day. Still, the only good thing about working on Christmas Day is that it'll hold off Mamie from bellyaching about me not puttin' up a tree."

"You don't never have a Christmas tree?"

"Not if I can help it," Grady said and sighed, remembering all the times Mamie and Jackie had practically begged him to go cut down a tree and drag it home on top of his car and build a frame to hold it up. But he always squirmed out of it somehow.

"Don't that little girl of yours ever want one?" Homer said, refusing to get off the subject.

"Well, sometimes, but not as much as Mamie does. Once Mamie made her a stocking to put on the fireplace and another time she fixed up some possumhaw on the mantelpiece. And then I brought in an armload of mistletoe I picked off of that bunch of scrub oaks out on the road to Rowena. That seemed to satisfy Jackie, but Mamie is always at me. I know it will come some day, but I am holding out the best I can."

"And you holding out satisfies Mamie, does it?" Homer still wouldn't leave it alone.

"I didn't say that, did I?" Grady made a face. "Mamie's always at me to go out to Henry's and cut her a cedar for a Christmas tree. Old J. B. Adams always has a tree that looks like it come out of Sanger Brothers Department Store down in Dallas. She wants me to put up one just like his."

"And you ain't gonna do it?"

"Not till I have to," Grady said, "but it's beginning to look like I can't hold out more than another Christmas or two. Jackie's four now, and I figure by the time Mamie has another year to work on her, the two of them will wear me down."

"And then I guess you'll have to put up a tree."

"Ha! I guess I will. Wouldn't you?"

Homer laughed, too, and said, "Who wears the britches in your family?"

Grady said, "Well, Homer, I wouldn't like to say I did. My daddy always said, 'A feller who claims to be boss at home will lie about other stuff.'"

"Yeah, I reckon so," Homer laughed as Grady drove off.

It was nearly four o'clock when Grady got back to the Bodark Springs Post Office, and it was four thirty before he checked in his money orders and registered mail slips, put up the mail he couldn't deliver, and looked in his pigeon holes at the mail that had come in late.

It was starting to get dark when Grady Dell headed north on Center Street in his three-year-old Chevrolet 490. He and Mamie and Jackie lived in a four-room house sitting on a slight rise out on the north edge of Bodark Springs. Grady always backed the fifty yards from the road to the house so the car would be headed down the hill. It saved cranking, he said; all he had to do was let the Chevy roll a few yards, throw it into second gear, let out the clutch, and let it jerk to a start on compression.

Every day when he got home from his route—usually two hours earlier than today—Jackie would run from the house to the car screaming at the top of her voice, "Daddy's home! Daddy's home!" She always cried it over and over until she got to the car and Grady grabbed her and held her high over his head. But today there wasn't a sound from the house. The lights were on, but he couldn't see any movement inside. He quickened his pace across the swept, packed-dirt yard.

"What if . . . ?" he said half aloud, but he couldn't finish the sentence containing the vague fear that always edged into his mind when he came home. Before he could think of a disaster to scare him, the door opened, and Jackie and Mamie stood looking at him as if he held the keys to all human happiness.

"We got us a tree, Daddy! A tree! We got us a tree!" Jackie screamed as she jumped up and down in the doorway.

Oh, Lord, thought Grady, now I'll have to drive back into town to the Ben Franklin store to get icicles and tinsel rope for that damned tree.

"When did y'all get it up?" Grady asked. And then, "Who put it up for you? Where'd you get the tree in the first place?" He asked his third question and paused for breath. He couldn't make head nor tail of the jumble of words that Jackie began pouring out. The only words that he heard over and over again were "Uncle Henry."

So, he thought, my danged brother has cut down a cedar and brought it over for them to have a Christmas tree. I guess Mamie must have nagged him the way she has nagged me for four years. But that still don't keep me from having to drive back into Bodark to get icicles and an angel and Lord knows whatnot to put on it.

Grady looked up, shrugged his shoulders and said, "Well,

y'all get your coats on and let's go back into town to the Ben Franklin's to get some ornaments for Henry's tree."

"We already got 'em, Daddy! We got 'em!" Jackie screeched out, grating on Grady's nerves—nerves frayed by the long hours of the Christmas mail rush.

Mamie hadn't said a word throughout all this commotion.

"Well," Grady said, trying not to let an edge creep into his voice, "let's go in and see how you all have decorated your tree."

"It ain't up yet." These were Mamie's first words.

"Ain't up yet?" Grady asked, "What do you mean 'ain't up'?"

"I mean it ain't been put up. And the first thing you'll have to do is build a stand to put it on. And you better get started because J. B. Adams is going to walk down here when he gets his decorated about nine o'clock and see how you done with yours." Mamie said all this in one breath.

"And how does J. B. Adams know we got a tree anyway?" Grady was starting to edge toward the door to get in out of the cold.

"I told Mrs. Adams when I walked up there to borrow some ornaments off of them. And Mrs. Adams, she said, 'J. B.'s been waiting for four years to see you put up a Christmas tree.'"

Telling the Adamses about the tree that Henry had brought was Mamie's way of making sure Grady put up the tree. Now she had him trapped for sure.

"And how am I supposed to make a stand for this tree?"

"I guess you are gonna have to bust up that big packing box that the icebox come in and use them two-by-fours for a stand." Mamie had it all figured. Now she was smiling.

"All right," Grady was resigned. "Let's have a look at this li'l old tree that your Uncle Henry has cut."

"It ain't little, Daddy! It ain't little!" Jackie said.

"Okay, baby, let's see this big ol' tree then," Grady said and ran his hand through her hair. It can't be too hard, he thought, but I sure hate to spend Christmas Eve messin' with a damned tree.

Grady Dell was sparing in his use of profanity. Except when Homer made him mad or when the Chevy got stuck in the mud on his route, he tried to keep his language clean. Even in his most secret thoughts he had avoided it ever since he got out of the Argonne Forest in 1918. He had seen and heard too much that was violent and nasty. So he resolved to drop army talk and army ways as soon as he got home from the war.

But when he saw the tree, he said, "Jesus Christ!" It slipped out before he could stop it.

"Grady!" Mamie screamed.

"Daddy! Daaaddy!" shouted Jackie.

Grady had walked almost across the living room before he spotted the seven-foot tree that Mamie said Henry had cut and put in the second room in the little shotgun house.

"Jeeeeesus Christ!" This time under his breath. A whisper.

"Mamie! Just how do you think—" He stopped and tried to remember all the things he had promised himself when he had married Mamie five years before. She had been sixteen and he had been thirty-two when they got married. She is still just a kid, he thought, and just because I'm getting old, I shouldn't take it out on her and Jackie.

While he had been thinking, Mamie had been talking. "And so that's all there is to it," she finished the sentence that he had not heard the first part of.

"What?"

Mamie repeated what she had said, "I said that all you have to do is make a stand, brace it up good, and put it in that corner over by the stove." She pointed with her chin at the Warm Morning heater that stood in front of the sealed-up fireplace that was all the heat the house had when they moved in. Mamie said she couldn't stand to live where all they had was fireplace heat. So Grady had borrowed twenty dollars from Henry and another twenty-five from the bank. Then he had Thurmond Whitmire from Eastis County Furniture come out and put it in. When Mamie asked Grady why he didn't just order the stove from Sears and Roebuck or Monkey Ward and put it in himself, he told her, "Because I ain't handy."

And now this, he thought.

"I ain't handy!" He had told her that a thousand times, but he told her again tonight, "Mamie you know how unhandy I am. I doubt I could ever make a tree like that stand up. That thing'll fall and kill somebody if I try to put it up."

"It won't do no such of a thing! If J. B. Adams can make one stand up, so can you!" Mamie figured that since J. B. was a bookkeeper for the T&P Railroad, he had to be less adept at carpentry than Grady, who had been raised on a farm. Grady never could convince her that being raised on a farm didn't necessarily make you handy with a hammer.

"Didn't you ever have to fix nothing when you lived out there near Windom with your momma and them?"

The "and them" were his father and his brothers Henry and Grover. Tonight she was explaining to Grady as if he were a child, so she said, "Your momma and them." She usually ran it together and said, "Your mommanem."

"Nope, I left all that fixing to Henry. He was the handy one. Grover was the strong one. I was the one that left the farm and took a job." He almost said, "And I was the one that married you." But he didn't.

He said, "Henry is as handy as the pocket on a shirt and could put this thing up in ten minutes, but I'll probably break a damned arm fooling with it."

"No you won't. Why don't you get the hammer and start bustin' up that crate while I get your supper on the table."

It was always "his supper."

It was as if she and Jackie did not eat with him but stood behind his chair to serve him "his" meals. The truth of it was that Grady cooked more than Mamie, who was often abed with one of her "jumping" headaches.

While Mamie put "his supper" on the table, Grady went out to the garage that was not a garage but a storehouse and barked two knuckles breaking up the packing box. He found a rusted saw that had belonged to his father—a fair hand at carpentry—and cut the two-by-fours into two-foot lengths. He thought, Well, maybe it won't be so hard. I'll just make an X for a base, and then I use four of these pieces to steady the tree on the X.

So, in a considerably better spirit, Grady went back into the house carrying his six short lengths of wood and thinking, This can't be too hard to do. If old J. B. Adams, who walks like he's got a cob stuck up his ass, can do it, I guess I can.

So after eating his supper, Grady went into the living room to put the tree up before J. B. could get his set up and decorated. He knew J. B. would finish about nine o'clock and then walk the quarter mile to the Dell house.

An hour later, Grady had his X made, but he had no luck getting the seven-foot tree to stand up. Mamie and Jackie had held it at first and had dropped it on him three times while he tried to put the base on. Then he tried to steady it by leaning it in the corner while he pounded nail after nail into the base of the tree. But by eight thirty, the trunk of the cedar looked as if it had been shot with a twelve-gauge shotgun. Grady then sawed off some bottom limbs and some of the trunk and tried again. He thought about cutting off half of the tree and seeing if he could turn the big tree into one about three feet high.

But Jackie started to cry and Mamie said, "I ain't gonna be shamed before the Adamses. If you'd wanted to, you could of put that tree up for this baby's Christmas."

By this time, Grady had stopped talking altogether. But he was thinking furiously. And he thought, it ain't no baby that you are worrying about. It's showing off in front of them Adamses. It's getting me to do something that I don't want to do. It's making me look like a fool that you want. But, as always, he kept his mouth shut.

By nine thirty, Mamie had figured out that she had better leave the living room and get as far away from Grady as she could. He still wasn't talking, and his lips had lost all color. He had broken out in a total and complete sweat. He wasn't even mumbling now—and hadn't mumbled since eight forty-five. He was dead quiet. And he was pounding nail after nail into the helpless trunk of the cedar.

At ten o'clock, Grady went to the window to look across the field to J. B. Adams's house. Just as he pulled the curtains back, he saw the Adamses' porch light come on.

"Well, I-God, old J. B. can walk across that field and down that street and right through these two back yards if he wants to, but he ain't gonna see no damned Xmas tree standing in this living room," mumbled Grady. And then a thought hit him that was simplicity itself.

Mamie heard the front door slam. In a few minutes she heard it slam again, and then she heard a banging from the front room that seemed as if it would break every window in the house. "Oh, my God," she said out loud, "what if he's lost his mind? What if he got some of that shell shock from the war? What if he comes back here with that claw hammer and kills me and this baby?"

"Mamie!" Grady screamed her name from the front room.

"Mamie! You and Jackie get them ornaments and come up here right now! Yonder comes J. B. Adams, and I want this tree decorated before he gets here!

"—Come on! Now! I mean NOW! Y'hear me?"

Mamie and Jackie rushed into the room to find the tree standing upright and filling the corner of the room. Without thinking, Mamie quickly put on the one strand of lights that they had borrowed and started hooking ornaments. Round and round the tree Grady looped the threaded popcorn strands that Mamie had made earlier in the day. Jackie threw the icicles as she jumped up and down and ran around the tree following Grady's placing of the popcorn rope. They got the lights plugged in just as J. B. Adams knocked on the door. Mamie had had no time to look at the tree before she ran to the door to let J. B. in.

When J. B. got his coat off and started to admire the tree (he was too polite not to admire it), Mamie began to puzzle out what J. B. had seen immediately.

She noticed the tree move, sway slightly. She thought, "It ain't swaying from the top, it's swaying from the bottom!"

She said in a loud voice, "Grady, you've h—!" But she caught herself, and instead of finishing the word she started, she stuttered, "hhhurt your hand!"

He said, "It ain't hurt!" and turned to say something to J. B. Adams about the fireworks that were beginning to be fired off all over Bodark to celebrate Christmas.

Grady and J. B. lived as neighbors for a good many more years, and never once in all that time did either one—or Mamie or Grace Adams or Jackie or Mary Faith Adams or Archie Adams or anybody else—mention that when Grady saw J. B.'s porch light come on, he rushed out to the garage and grabbed a 20-penny nail and some baling wire and went tearing back into the living room. Then he took the nail and hammered it into the pine ceiling and hung the tree by baling wire. When he had finished, and before he had called Mamie and Jackie out to decorate the tree, he whispered violently to himself, "I-God, now there's your damned Xmas tree! I hope to God you have a merry damned Xmas!" Pronouncing the X rather than saying Christmas made him feel a whole lot better.

TWO

Mr. George's Joint

1936

The battered sign on the unpainted shack on Railroad Avenue in Bodark Springs said:

Mr. George's Joint
Coloreds Onlie

The only customer at three thirty on a Thursday afternoon in the spring of 1936 was Grady Dell, the rural letter carrier, who sat drinking from a bottle of Hudepohl. The sign may have said "Coloreds Onlie," but Grady was white.

"You want another bottle of beer, Mr. Grady?"

"I guess so, George, if you've got another Hudepohl. I can just about manage just one more beer before I have to head on home."

"Hudepohl is what I got plenty of. Hudepohl and Burger is all I sell. I don't carry no white folkses' beer, and since you near about the only white man that comes in here, I hope you can make out with what I stock. Niggers won't pay the extra nickel for Schlitz and Budweiser and Pabst. So I just stock this Cincinnati beer at a dime apiece. For awhile I carried Oertles '92, but couldn't nobody pronounce it, so I went back to Hudepohl and Burger."

"And nobody has trouble saying Hudepohl?"

"Oh, naw, they just calls it 'huddie pole.'"

"George, how come a colored man calls his customers niggers? And how come sometimes you sound white and sometimes colored?"

"I don't know that I does. Sound white I mean. Must be associatin' with the quality like you and sometimes with a bunch of niggers. That's what they are, Mr. Grady. Most of them. I don't get many colored preachers and deacons and schoolteachers in here. I just get old deadbeat niggers wanting me to put beer on the cuff. They say, 'Mr. George, I pay you Sattidy or Sattidy week sho.'"

"I guess the coloreds are worse off than the whites, but God knows everybody is having hard times. These are the worst times I can remember, George. Real hard times."

"Yessir, I know that. If I hadn't made a good bit back in during the war when cotton was high and niggers and whites both could make out, I couldn't stay in business. Now I am barely gettin' by selling a little barbecue to white folks and the beer my niggers buy when they get their welfare checks. 'Course some of them are 'drawing their pennies' from the unemployment office after being laid off from the coal mines and the railroad yards and the cotton gin. And all them checks is mighty little nowdays."

George Moore was said to be the richest colored man in Bodark Springs, probably in Northeast Texas. He was rumored to sell more than a few bottles of beer on Saturday night and lots of barbecue to white folks. Some said George had about twenty colored men running stills all along both sides of the Red River in Eastis and Fannin Counties and over in Bryan County, Oklahoma. People said George Moore got rich during Prohibition selling white whiskey as far east as Texarkana and as far west as Dallas and Fort Worth.

Nobody in Bodark knew for sure how much whiskey George Moore sold, for he was strict about not selling any at all in Eastis and Fannin counties. White men had that all sewed up, and even though George was well liked by whites and blacks alike, he knew better than to poach on the cartels of Tubby Wallace and half-a-dozen white men who sold both moonshine and bonded whiskey in Eastis and Fannin counties.

George may have been rich, but if he was he didn't keep it in banks in Bodark or anywhere else anybody could find. And he didn't live high. He had a room in back of his beer joint and drove a 1929 Model A Ford coupe. But he must have had something going, for about twice a year, he would close his beer joint for two weeks and disappear from sight. Nobody ever saw him leave town, and nobody ever saw him come back. He didn't take his car. He left it sitting behind his cafe all the time he was gone. Max, over at the T&P station, swore that George never left or returned on the train, and Shorty Holloway, the Greyhound driver, checked with all his bus-driving friends and said nobody ever saw George get on a bus. Boyd McGlothin, the house painter who had lots of theories about George's life, always said, "I bet somebody come from Dallas and picked him up after he had walked a mile or two out of town. Or maybe he might of caught the late-night freight and rode the rails to Texarkana."

But nobody knew.

Boyd was pretty sure it was the mysterious white wife who came and got him. If there was a white wife. One rumor running in the quarters said that George had gone off to Mexico and married a white woman that he kept somewhere in Dallas. That he had two or three part-white children. Since George was light skinned, some said maybe his white-woman children were "passing." But nobody ever knew for sure or saw George in Dallas or anywhere but Bodark.

"Yeah," Boyd McGlothin said, "I hear old George Moore has got a 1936 Cadillac car somewhere in Dallas and a wife that buys her clothes at Neiman and Marcus."

None of the blacks ever asked George where he went when he closed or what he did for a month out of every year. Old Melvin Spruille, the postmaster, once asked him about his trips out of town, and George went all Uncle Remus and said, "Well suh, I goes up to Chicago to see my tooth dentist and to study the Old Testa-Mint with some rabbis I knows up there in what them Jews calls 'the windy city.'" Then he grinned and flashed the gold tooth that had a small diamond in the middle of it. That gold tooth seemed to be George Moore's only vanity. Nobody in Bodark ever saw him in anything but threadbare khaki pants, a blue work shirt, and a straw farmer's hat when he went outside.

George usually closed and disappeared late in November and again in July or August. George was gone in 1936 by August fifteenth. When it got to be early in September, people started going by George's joint and banging on the door. By the end of September, even white people began to worry that something had happened to George Moore. October came and went, and by November the whole town decided that George Moore was dead. His bootleggers up along the Red claimed that they had not heard from him, and some of the white bootleggers were making noises about raiding George's stills if they could find them.

Early in December everything went to hell in Bodark Springs and people started to forget about George Moore.

First, "Crip" Lundy went crazy and had to be sent to Wichita Falls to the insane asylum.

Then Tommy Earl Dell got kidnapped.

And then Reavy Lee got out of prison after serving four years for the murder of Thelma Todd, his common-law wife.

No wonder George Moore's disappearance got shuffled aside.

Here is how things fell out in the late fall of the year of our Lord 1936.

Crip Lundy had got infantile paralysis not many years after Franklin D. Roosevelt made infantile paralysis famous. Crip was not only partially paralyzed, but he had a fierce case of grand mal epilepsy. And on top of that he was mean as a cottonmouth moccasin. He used his crutches to trip people walking down the sidewalks of Bodark. He swung his leg braces at little kids in school and sent a few of them to Dr. Clayton's clinic. He had been a trial to Gladys Lundy, the Avon lady, all his life, with his fits and his paralysis and his meanness. Gladys walked all over town ringing doorbells and selling hand cream and other delights to the women who could afford cosmetics in these hard times. Crip, whose real name was Randall, worked off and on for Old Man Todd the peanut and popcorn man. But sometimes when he was manning the popcorn machine, he would have an epileptic seizure and have to be held down by passersby until he came to himself. Then he was weak and stunned and somebody had to go find Gladys to take him home.

Old Man Todd (nobody could remember his first name) had a popcorn wagon with bicycle wheels on it. He usually parked it outside Harry Isadore's Dry Goods and Notions and plugged his popper into Harry's electrical outlet. He sold popcorn and hot peanuts for a dime a bag. And when times were as hard as they were in the thirties, a big bag of popcorn might feed four or five hungry kids on the way to the movie house next to what people called "the Jew store." How Crip helped Mr. Todd nobody could ever figure out. He just seemed to stand around and devil little kids. Then one Saturday, Crip had more than a seizure. He started screaming and poured hot oil all over Mr. Todd. Then he broke out the window of the dry goods store with his crutches and started screaming, "Jew! Jew! Goddamn Jew!" at Harry Isadore.

Orr Starnes, the chief of police, had to hold Crip down and put handcuffs on him. Crip never recognized his mother again and spent day after day in the city jail screaming words that nobody could understand. Some said he was possessed by the devil, and some said he had been taken over by God and was talking in tongues like the Holy Rollers did. Dr. Clayton said, "No, he is not possessed. He is just batshit crazy." Dr. Clayton got him committed to Wichita Falls, and that was the last anybody ever saw of Crip Lundy. Gladys was sad for a while, but it was not long before she felt the relief that everybody else in Bodark did.

And then Tommy Earl Dell got kidnapped. That proved what Mamie Dell always predicted would happen to him. Mamie knew as soon as the Lindbergh baby was kidnapped in 1932 that Tommy Earl was next in line for a kidnapping and ransom demand and eventual murder. Grady tried to reason with her, but she said, "I just know. Somebody is going to kidnap my baby just like they done that little Lindbergh baby."

Grady said, "Mamie, Charles Lindbergh was rich. Nobody is going to kidnap a mail carrier's boy. Hell, I make $125 a month. What kind of ransom could I pay?"

"I know it! I just know it! I can feel it! Somebody is after my baby. And you are gonna let some maniac get him and torture him to death. And then I will have to take his little dead body and bury it my ownself!"

When Mamie had to go to Sherman to the sinus doctor or to Paris to the chiropractor or to Dallas to the kidney specialist, she never left Tommy Earl with Rosie Maubry or her sister Modell Floyd. She had to have a big man to guard her baby. So Grady got Rendon Maubry, Rosie's brother, to come and guard little Tommy Earl. Rendon had been laid off from the rock quarry for a year or two and was glad to get any work he could. Even being a bodyguard to a small child.

Mamie still fretted. "I know somebody is gonna steal my baby and take him away and torture him to death and I am gonna have to—"

"Mamie," Grady interrupted, "Nobody is going to steal that baby, and if they do there will be a dead nigger laying there. Rendon must go six foot five and weigh 260 pounds, and if he can't protect that baby, Police Chief Orr Starnes and the whole Texas National Guard can't."

Four years later, when Tommy Earl turned up missing, Mamie was vindicated. She screamed and cried and said, "I tried to tell you, but you wouldn't listen to me! Now you are going to pay whatever they ask for that baby. I don't care if you have to sell your soul to the devil. If you don't, I can see my precious baby somewhere laying a corpse."

Grady mumbled that he didn't know how to get ahold of the devil or he would. But he doubted that his soul would bring the price of a pint of Four Roses blended whiskey. He was at least as worried as Mamie, but he knew screaming and taking on wouldn't get the boy back. First, he called Orr Starnes and then he got Dr. Clayton to come and give Mamie a shot. For the rest of the night he walked the floor and managed to do away with that half a pint of Four Roses he figured his soul was worth.

While Tommy Earl was still missing, the whole town had a new scandal. Reavy Lee was out of prison. Four years before, he had killed Thelma Todd and got sent to Huntsville for a life sentence. Now he was back in the county somewhere.

Charlie Stone, the mail clerk, said, "I heard Reavy Lee had got out because he had become a Holy Roller preacher down on the Ellis Farm."

Melvin Spruille said, "That's crazy. They don't let murderers out just because they get a dose of religion. What was he doing on the Ellis Farm? I thought they kept the worst of them in 'The Walls' down at Huntsville."

"Well, you know they work them convicts out on the farms and guard them with men on horseback. With dogs and shotguns. It's probably worse than making license plates or whatever they do in Huntsville."

Jack Hurst, the only Republican in Bodark, was listening at the window of the post office and said, "Probably that Democrat you all elected, old Jimmy Allred, pardoned him. They do that you know."

Reavy didn't get pardoned, and he didn't seem to be on parole. He was just out. And Max over at the T&P station told Burt Curlee that he was up near Telephone in Fannin County. "He is preaching and talking in tongues in some little jackleg Pentecostal Holiness church."

Since people heard that Reavy was out of prison, all the talk in town turned to how Reavy had killed Thelma one Saturday back in 1932 and then turned the shotgun on himself.

Gladys Lundy had seen the killing, and she got to tell the story over and over when it happened. Now, she had to tell it again. And again and again. But that suited her fine.

"Well, I was walking down Railroad Avenue delivering some Avon cosmetics to Mrs. Holley when I saw it all happen. Mrs. Holley always orders the best products Avon sells, and even if it was a Saturday and I am usually off, I took her stuff as soon as it come in on the T&P. She had some cold cream, some foundation, a tube of Tahiti Blush lipstick, and I can't remember what all else."

Tarp Davidson, who had heard this story fifty times but never tired of it, interrupted and said, "So what did you see, Gladys? Did you actually see Reavy shoot Thelma right off of that front porch at Old Man Todd's?"

"I sure did. He had that shotgun aimed at her and said, 'If I can't have you, ain't nobody going to!' He said it about three times—maybe four—and then he shot her and she fell offen the porch into the yard. I didn't know whether to shit or go blind. I just stood there froze like a icicle."

"And then what? You saw Reavy shoot hisself?"

"That's right. He takened that big old long-barrel shotgun and pointed it at his own head and with his left hand he fumbled around with the trigger and then *blam*! That gun went off and Reavy fell down on the ground. I knowed he was dead, so I run to Clinkscales Barber Shop to call Orr Starnes."

Gladys ran to the shop, called the Powers Cafe and told Ralph Powers to run out and tell Chief Starnes that two people were dead down on Railroad Avenue. Starnes usually sat parked at the curb by the cafe on Saturday afternoons in case a scuffle broke out or somebody came speeding down Main Street for the chief to chase down and ticket. When he heard the news from Ralph, he hollered across the street to Old Man Todd and told him to head home.

Gladys never got over Old Man Todd's leaving her boy Crip, who was in the middle of a grand mal seizure, to run home and see about his folks. She said, "He just left Randall laying there in the middle of a fit. He could of swallowed his tongue and died for all Old Man Todd cared. I mean, I blame him for all that led to Randall having to lose his mind and be sent to Wichita Falls."

Burt Curlee, who was listening to Gladys tell her story for the fifth time that day, said, "But that shootin' was about four years before Crip—I mean Randall—had to go off to the asylum, wasn't it?"

Gladys bristled and said, "Burt Curlee, you don't know nothing about it. Randall had nothing but nightmares and fits for all them years after Old Man Todd left him laying there in the street in front of the Jew store nearly dying."

Despite what Gladys thought she saw, Reavy didn't die. He managed to blow off his right ear and scar up the side of his face from the shotgun blast. Orr Starnes took him to jail, a trial was held later in the year, and Reavy Lee was sentenced to life in prison in the state penitentiary in Huntsville.

Melvin Spruille said, "And now, in the year of our Lord nineteen and thirty-six, that fool Reavy Lee is out of prison and trying to preach. Hell, he can't read and write. How is he going to tell them ignorant bootleggers up on the Red what the Bible says?"

Nobody knew the answer to that, and nobody much cared. All the talk was still about the kidnapping of Tommy Earl Dell.

Except that Tommy Earl hadn't been kidnapped.

One day after Tommy had been missing for four days, Grady, still off work and looking everywhere for his boy, was driving down Railroad Avenue near where Old Man Todd lived when he saw Rendon Maubry walking along holding Tommy Earl by the hand. Grady slammed on the brakes and jumped out of the car when he saw Rendon and the boy.

Grady didn't know what to say, so he just grabbed Tommy Earl and hugged him.

Rendon said, "Mr. Grady, didn't nobody steal that child. He just run off. He was down in the quarters looking for me when he got lost and hid out in the Macedonia Baptist Church."

"Looking for you? For what?"

"Well, what he told the Reverend Washington, the new preacher down there, was that his momma—Miss Mamie—had whipped him pretty bad the day he run off. She took a belt to him, he said, and then she went in the bedroom and went to sleep. Jackie was at school, so he just left home looking to find me. He said he wanted to be colored like me."

"Did he say why? I mean except that he was mad at Mamie?"

"Well, sir, I don't know how to put this, but he said he was tired of being a white child and wanted to be a colored boy and live with me. Only he didn't know where I stay, so he got tired and slipped in the Macedonia Church, which was open. It stay open all the time since Reverend Woodrow Wilson Washington come to town to pastor them Baptists. Me, I am a member of the Ebenezer Church of God in Christ, so Reverend

Washington, who had just come here from down around Corsicana, didn't really know me or where I stay at. Anyway, I was gone out of town. I had walked over to Black Diamond Mines to see could I get on over there and couldn't of been found even if the reverend had known where I stayed."

Grady said, "How come that preacher didn't call the law when he found the boy?"

"Call the law! God knows what they would have done when they seen a nigger preacher with a white child that everybody said had been stole. The boy—little Tommy here—had crawled up behind the piano and had gone to sleep and the Reverend didn't see him till after he had been there all night. When he found him, he knew the police was looking for the boy, and he told me that if he turned him in, they would think he had stole that boy and some gang of white men would lynch him. And they might have. I even figured if somebody saw me bringing Tommy back into town, I might get lynched my ownself. But I love that little boy, and I didn't want you to keep on missing him the way you was. So I takened a chance and brought him back to town."

"Lord, Lord, Rendon. I can't believe anybody would ever think you had done anything to my boy."

"Oh, Mr. Grady, lots of peoples want to think niggers is killers and baby stealers. Worse than them gypsies that come through Bodark every summer."

"Rendon, I am much obliged to you for bringing him home. He looks about wore out. He hasn't said a word. Has he quit talking since he run off?"

"Nossir, he just ashamed of hisself is all."

Grady knelt down and hugged the boy and said, "Tommy Earl, I am going to take you home now, and I promise you one thing: your momma won't ever whip you again. Not as long as I live."

And she didn't.

And then he looked up at Rendon and said, "Has he had anything to eat in these four days?"

"Oh, yessir, the reverend and his wife fed him and put him in a real bed after they found him laying up under the piano. When the reverend found me after I got back from Black Diamond—where there wasn't no jobs—he told me that the little boy kept saying, 'I want Rendon to look after me.' Reverend Washington didn't know me since I goes to Ebenezer, but he found my sister Modell and she found me and sent me over to Macedonia Church where I found this child. He kept saying, 'I want to be colored like you, Rendon.'"

Grady said, "I guess he knows how good a man you are, Rendon. I do, and I appreciate all you have done for me and Tommy. He remembers all the times you stayed with him when I was taking Mamie all over to see doctors and chiropractors and faith healers."

"Yessir, well I said to him, 'Look at me, Tommy, I am black as a lump of number nine coal, and you are white as a sheet off the line. You can't never be colored, and if you knowed how it is to be colored, you would want to go back home to your momma and daddy.' And that's the God's own truth, Mr. Grady. Being colored gets harder and harder as times get harder and harder. Sometimes I think them slaves had it better than we do over here in the quarters."

Things simmered down in Bodark Springs for a while, but then Skip Griffin, the insurance man, came back from Dallas one day and told Grady Dell that he had seen George Moore driving up Preston Road in a big gray Cadillac V16.

Grady said, "What made you think it was George Moore? It could have been any big colored man working as a chauffeur for some rich white people. I am convinced that George is dead. Probably killed to get at the money he is supposed to have made off all that white whiskey people said he sold out of stills along the Red."

"Grady, I know George Moore as well as you ever did, even though I didn't hang out in his nigger joint drinking beer like you did."

"I still don't believe it was him you saw. I still say he is dead or he wouldn't have just disappeared like he did," Grady said.

"Well, I know what I saw," Skip said and walked off.

A week or so later, Ned Rew, whose brother had a wholesale electric business in Dallas, walked in the post office and told Charlie Stone, the window clerk, that he was pretty sure he had seen George Moore in Dallas driving some big old car, a Cadillac or a LaSalle or a Packard or something.

Charlie said, "Can't you tell the difference between a Cadillac and a Packard?"

"It ain't important what kind of big, underslung car I saw. What I am trying to tell you is that I saw George Moore that is supposed to be dead. George Moore, the big yellow nigger with the gold tooth. I saw him driving along slow up Preston Road, and I looked right at him. He looked at me, but he turned away quick like he had something to hide."

Grady Dell, who had been sorting his mail, came up to the window and asked, "Where on Preston Road did you see him?"

Ned said, "Why do you care where it was on Preston Road? Are you going over to Dallas to look for him?"

"No, I just wondered if it was close to where Skip Griffin said he saw him."

Ned said, "It was right where Preston crosses Mockingbird if you care. And I don't see why you would. Hell, at least he ain't here in Bodark Springs selling beer to white guys like you and running whiskey all over East Texas."

Ned stomped out, and Charlie said to Grady, "Do you reckon Skip and Ned are making up that story? They are cousins and might just be trying to fire up another rumor here in Bodark."

"That's probably right."

Melvin Spruille said, "It might be better if you men spent more time on post office business than on worrying about some dead nigger."

Things settled down in Bodark Springs. Reavy Lee never came into town. Tommy Earl was safe and seemed over his desire to be a colored child. Old Man Todd still ran the popcorn stand on Main Street, and Gladys Lundy still wore out shoe leather walking all over town selling Avon. Mr. George's Joint was still closed, and Grady Dell still carried the mail all over Eastis county and part of Fannin.

And then one night Grady's car broke down on his way back from Oklahoma where he had attended a VFW meeting. Grady couldn't get his old Ford with 60,000 miles on it to start, so he climbed into the back seat and decided to wait until some farmer came by on his way to town. Grady had had more than one drink up in Oklahoma, so sleep came deep and easy.

Sometime around four o'clock in the morning, somebody tapped on the passenger side back window. Grady turned over but stayed dead to the world. Then the noise grew loud and Grady woke up and looked out the window.

And saw George Moore.

"Jesus," Grady mumbled, "Jesus! What a damn nightmare! I must still be drunk to see a ghost way out here. Probably that bust-head Oklahoma whiskey."

"Nossiree, Mr. Grady, it ain't no ghost. It's just me. Old George Moore that everybody thought was dead."

When Grady finally realized it wasn't a dream, he opened the door and said, "George, I had about given up on you, even though Ned Rew and Skip Griffin said they had seen you in Dallas. I guess they were right."

"Yessir, they were I guess. I didn't see Mr. Skip, but I looked right at Mr. Ned Rew and hoped he wouldn't recognize me. I reckon he did though."

Grady said, "George, I can't tell you how glad I am that you are alive. But what are you doing out on these backroads in the middle of the night? Or are you dead and walking the earth like a natural man? You know, like it says in the Bible?"

"No, I am alive and not walking the earth. I have a car back there. I can give you a ride when you get good woke up."

Grady looked out the back window and saw the biggest, grayest, most underslung Cadillac he had ever seen.

"That must be the Cadillac V16 that Skip Griffin said he saw. Are you somebody's chauffeur down in Dallas now?"

"No. The car is mine. I posed as a chauffeur some, but my story is a whole lot stranger than that. If you want to hear it, and if you have got time to listen to an old nigger tell a strange tale, I will make your head swim worse than that Oklahoma rotgut whiskey. I wouldn't tell nobody but you, but you always treated me good. You about the only white man I ever liked in Bodark. You treated me just like I was anybody else."

Grady said, "You were never just anybody else to me. I guess the two men I like best in all of Eastis County—next to my brother Henry—were you and Rendon Maubry. Both colored men, neither one of them I would ever call a nigger. I do want to hear your story if you want to tell me. And I won't ever tell a soul if you don't want me to."

"Naw, you can tell anybody you want to, because I am pretty much gone from here for good."

Then George Moore told Grady how he had met a white woman when he was in the army in France in 1918 and they had gotten married.

"Was she a French woman?" Grady asked.

"No, she was from Dallas, Texas. I was a soldier and got shot up some, and she was a nurse with the Red Cross or the Salvation Army or something. We met in the hospital, and the next thing either one of us know, we had fell in love. I tried to tell her that we didn't have no future, but she insisted that we get married. Well, you know, we couldn't get married in the United States. That would have got me lynched for sure."

"So what they used to say was true. You all went off to Mexico and got married down there."

"Nossir, we was in Paris, and I had some leave after being wounded, so we went off to Lyons and got married. The French ain't too particular about whites and coloreds getting married. Then I got discharged, and we went back to Dallas to see what we could see. Well, you can imagine we didn't see anything for us as married folks. I moved up to Bodark and bought that joint with what I had saved and my mustering-out pay. We thought we could see each other a few times a year, and maybe someday we could find a way to live together. Her folks had a right smart of money and lived in Highland Park there in Dallas. Well, they thought she was a war widow and had married a Frenchman in Paris."

"Lord, God, George, that sounds like you all were in a helluva tight spot. What did her folks think when you showed up?"

"I didn't ever show up. Me and her had us two honeymoons a year, but far away from Dallas. You remember how I would disappear for a couple of weeks now and again?"

"I do. And some rumors said you had a white wife in Dallas and went off to be with her. I never believed that. At least I didn't back then."

"I don't know how that story got spread, but it was sort of true. We didn't meet in Dallas. I would shut up the beer joint and walk about two miles out of town and she would pick me up. Then I would be let off at the railroad station in Dallas and catch a train for Miami. She would catch the same train, but in the white people's car. Then we caught a boat for Havana, Cuba, and had us a honeymoon twice a year."

"That must have cost a lot for a man running a beer joint. I mean the trip to Cuba and all."

George said, "Well, her folks was rich, and before long I was, too. I guess you heard about them stills I had running up on the Red River, didn't you?"

"I heard, but I thought they were rumors like the white wife and the big car."

"Nossir, I had a bunch of veterans from the colored infantry making some good whiskey up there. It was not just the usual rotgut that lots of these white moonshiners make. My boys made good stuff. It was so good that I had a deal with Mr. Al Capone up in Chicago that paid me as much as $20,000 a year. Mr. Al said my liquor was nearly as good as what he could get from Canada."

"You must be rich then if you had all that going for you. That and the beer joint."

"Ha! That beer joint just about kept the light bill paid. Nossir, I made big money offen them stills. I guess if the truth was known, I may be the richest man in Northeast Texas. And it is all in banks in Cuba and in Dallas and in Miami under my real name."

Grady looked amazed. "Your real name?"

George smiled and said, "Yessir that was part of the deal. My wife used my real name, and I takened this George Moore name to keep anybody from tracking me down. Her folks liked my real name, which sounds sort of Frenchified. I hope you don't mind if I don't tell you what my real name is."

Grady smiled and said, "I don't want you to tell me anything you don't want to. I appreciate all you are telling me. I guess you trust me—at least a little."

"You the only white man I trust in Bodark. But I would like to keep my name secret partly because of the boys."

"You mean the boys who work for you up on the Red?"

George said, "Lord no. Not them boys. They are all scattered after tonight. I paid them off and they are going all over the country. I mean my boys, my children."

Grady was amazed again. "You and the lady in Dallas have children? How old?"

"Had children. My wife passed a few months ago. My twin boys are sixteen and never accepted that they had a nigger for a daddy. They are off in school. One is at Sewanee Military Academy in Tennessee and one is at the Kent School in Connecticut. They both Episcopal schools. My wife was Episcopal, you see. Her folks are long dead. They never knew about me. Thought she was a widow woman. The sister knows everything, and she is the one the boys stay with when they are not in school. She lives in Nashville.

"While my wife was sick, I had to dress up in this black suit and pretend to be her chauffeur. Her daddy's old chauffeur had a place over the garage that I pretended was where I slept. Then as she got really bad and had to have a nurse, I stayed up there all the time. I don't think nobody ever figured out that I was more than a driver. If they had, I probably wouldn't be here now. Them white folks in Highland Park are dead against niggers unless they got uniforms on."

"I hate to ask this," Grady said, "but is it hard on the boys being part colored and going to those white schools?"

"No. They don't look colored. I'm pretty light skinned, and their mother was a pure blond. So the boys look a little like they might be what my wife told her folks they was—part French like her dead husband that never existed.

"Well, Mr. Grady, I'm gonna drive on past your house a ways and let you out so everybody think you are walking in from a ways off. Then I am going to drive back to Dallas where I have a buyer for this car. After that, I guess I will go to Cuba and old George Moore will be as dead as you all thought he was for the last few months."

A few days after George dropped Grady off, Ned Rew came by Powers Cafe where Grady was drinking a Budweiser and said,

"Have you heard any more about old George Moore? I been back to Highland Park several times hoping to see him in that big old car, but I can't catch sight of him."

Grady took the last swig from the Budweiser and said, "Aw, hell, Ned, you didn't see George Moore in the first place. It was some other nigger driving a big old limousine. George Moore could barely drive that old A-Model he had."

Ned said, "I guess I know what I saw."

"No," Grady said, "you never saw George Moore. I know for a fact that George Moore is dead."

THREE

A Blue and Gray Christmas

1937

Granny Dell married in 1880 and moved to Texas.

It looked to her like everybody in Alabama had either moved to Texas or was going to. She hated to leave the only home she had ever known, but Jim, her husband, said East Texas was better cotton country than Shelby County, Alabama. So they bought a secondhand Studebaker wagon, hitched the two mules to it, and made their torturous way across Mississippi and Louisiana.

Jim's cousin had settled in Red River County near Bogota, but Jim and Jerusha had to move west to sharecrop on a farm in Eastis County until 1890, when they managed to save enough to buy a hardscrabble farm over near Windom in Fannin County. It was better than Shelby County, but it never made as much cotton as Jim had read about in the brochures sent east from Texas, or that his cousin had written him about all through the seventies.

All three of Jim and Jerusha's sons were born on the little farm and began figuring out ways to get off it as soon as possible. Henry, the oldest, never made it and ended up running the farm Jim and Jerusha had finally managed to buy. Grover moved to Sherman and got a job on the railroad, and Grady served in the First Division in World War I and never went back to the farm after he got out of the Army of Occupation in 1919. He took the civil service exam, and, with his points as a veteran, got a job as a rural letter carrier out of Bodark Springs.

Jim Dell got killed in 1923 when his mules ran away with his wagon. He and his cousin Hudson were headed into Savoy when the mules got spooked. Uncle Hut, the name Hudson always went by after Jim died, got tangled up in two old straight chairs he and Jim used instead of a wagon seat, and lived to tell the story. He said Jim tried to jump for it and hit his head on a rock. He died that same day about five thirty in the afternoon.

Jerusha spent the rest of her life living with Henry and his wife Flora Irene on the farm that she and Jim had owned. She got old before her time, and by the time Tommy Earl, Grady's son, was old enough to remember, she was a bent old woman who looked like the Cherokee Indian everybody said she was. Tommy Earl always spent Christmas with her and his uncle and aunt and pestered Granny Dell to tell him about what he called "the old days."

Granny's old days were different from the ones Tommy Earl wanted to hear about. He wanted to know how it was when his daddy was a boy his age, but Granny's old days were long behind her and didn't include the Texas she had come to half a century before. When her grandson pestered her about "the old days," her mind took her back to her girlhood and young womanhood in Alabama. Texas had always been a mystery to her, even after more than forty years under the Lone Star. So when Tommy wanted stories about his daddy and his uncles, she always went back to a time nobody but her recalled.

The Christmas Eve when Tommy was five, Granny told him about the first Christmas Eve she could remember. He recalled it years later. Somehow, he remembered every word of her first

Christmas memory. He could never exactly say why it made such an impression, but he could remember it word for word years and years later.

Here is how he always told it. And he used her words.

It was the Christmas of eighteen and sixty-four. I was four and a half. I can't remember anything before that Christmas Eve. But I remember it just like it was yesterday. By then, the Yankees had already killed my daddy. I don't even remember him. Momma says he got wounded at Vicksburg in eighteen and sixty-three and caught pneumonia and died.

It was about four o'clock on Christmas Eve when the Yankees came. I don't remember how many there were, but it looked like the whole yard was full of them before we even knew they were there. I remember how cold it was. Momma and Helon and I were huddled up around the fireplace when we heard the horses.

Momma said, "It's the Yankees! You girls get under the bed! Quick!"

Before I could move, the door flew open and a Yankee soldier was standing in the room with us. Momma stood up. Helon dove under the bed. I looked at the Yankee soldier a long time; then I got behind Momma.

"Tell the other little girl to come out from under the bed," the Yankee said.

"Are you going to kill us?" Momma asked the soldier.

I began to cry. Helon, who was six, came out from under the bed and said, "Are you the Yankee who killed my daddy?"

Helon remembered Daddy. All I could remember about him was a smell, and I smelled that smell on the Yankee soldier. I don't know how to describe it—sort of like tobacco smoke mixed with a horse smell. Of course, by that time of the war, we didn't have a horse. Not even a mule. Our mule had been stole not long after my daddy went off to war, so I didn't even remember mule smell. It was only later that I could connect my daddy's smell and the Yankee soldier's smell with the smell of horses.

I knew it wasn't a cow smell. We still had a cow, but Momma kept Old Blossom hidden down in the woods so the Yankees and the traitors couldn't find her. Momma always slipped down across the creek and milked the cow before it got light in the morning or after it got dark at night. Momma hardly ever let Helon or me go near the cow, and she told us never to mention the cow to anybody because somebody would surely steal her.

I knew the Yankees had come to steal Old Blossom. And then they would kill Momma and then Helon and then me. Me last because I was the littlest.

But I was sure they would kill me.

I started to cry.

The Yankee stepped out on the porch and told the men to go into the barn and see if we had any hay or fodder for the horses.

"We don't," Momma said. "Somebody stole our mule just after the war started. We haven't made a crop since my husband went off to the war."

The Yankee told the men to go look in the barn anyway. When they started traipsing down to the barn, he hollered out to one of them and said, "Sergeant, keep the men in the barn out of this cold till I come and get you."

The Yankee came into the house and stood in front of the fire. "This fire feels good. Do you mind if I stay in here awhile and warm up? I have been in the saddle for two days, and I don't think I have ever been this cold."

"Did you kill our daddy?" Helon asked the man again.

"Momma, when is he going to kill us?" I had seen Momma shoot squirrels and rabbits and once a deer, and I knew the Yankee would shoot us and blood would run all over the floor of our house.

"I'm not going to kill you girls—or you either, Ma'am."

Momma seemed to be thinking hard. She said, "We don't have enough food to feed all your men, and what we have is pretty sorry, but I can give you some cornbread and buttermi—" Momma stopped. Later on, she told us that she knew for sure that the Yankee would torture us till he found out where our cow was and then kill the cow.

But the soldier didn't seem to notice that Momma had let the cat out of the bag. All he said was, "Ma'am, that would be nice. I would like that a lot."

When she went into the lean-to kitchen of our two-room house, she told us to stay near the fire. I knew she wanted us to watch the Yankee and see when he was going to shoot us.

The soldier sat in the rocking chair by the fire and Helon and I stood off to one side—watching. He turned toward us and said, "Are you girls ready for Christmas?"

We looked at each other. Neither of us had ever heard the word "Christmas." Momma told us later that she had never mentioned Christmas to us because since Daddy had gone off, she didn't have anything to give us. With Daddy off in the war and now dead, she said she didn't want to think about holidays and happy times.

The soldier asked us again, "Are you girls ready for Christmas?"

Momma came back into the room carrying a glass of buttermilk and a piece of cornbread on a plate. She handed them to the Yankee and said, "I never told my girls about Christmas. We have nearly starved to death since their daddy went off to the war, and I didn't think it was good to get their hopes up about pleasant times. We won't ever have them again."

"These little girls have never had a Christmas gift?"

"No," Momma said, "and it's mean of you to put the idea in their heads."

"I'm sorry," the man said, "but since I brought it up, maybe I should give them something for Christmas if that's all right." And he reached into his overcoat pocket and pulled out two bright red apples.

Momma said, "Did you steal the apples from some poor farmer on the way here?"

"No, ma'am, my wife sent them to me from Cade's Cove in East Tennessee. A man in my company got wounded and went on leave, and when he came back, he brought me some apples from my own trees."

Momma looked puzzled, "What are you doing in that blue uniform if you are from Tennessee?"

He said, "East Tennessee didn't vote to secede, so I got called up in the army. I haven't killed anybody yet, and I won't kill any Southerners if I can help it."

Helon had moved closer to the Yankee. She said, "Are you going to kill us?"

"No," the soldier said, "I have two little girls about the age of you two girls. I would never kill you, and I hope no Rebel soldier would think of killing them."

He turned to Momma and said, "I miss my girls, and it really makes me sad that here it is Christmas Eve and I can't be with them. When I saw your little girls, I thought of my two at home. That's why I asked if I could come in and sit by the fire awhile. They make me think of Helen and Elizabeth."

He looked at Helon and then at me, "What are your names?"

Helon said, "My name is Helon." We pronounced it Hee-lon, but it was the same name as one of his little girls Momma told us later.

I hid behind Momma's skirt again.

Momma told him my name: "Jerusha," she said.

The Yankee looked at me and said, "Jerusha. That's a pretty name. Is it from the Bible?"

I hid behind Momma again. What if he did shoot me? If he shot Momma and Helon first and saved me for last, I wouldn't want to live without them. And Daddy was already dead. So I came out from behind Momma and stood in front of the soldier. He handed me one of the apples and said, "Happy Christmas, Jerusha. And you, too Helen—I mean Helon." He gave her the other apple.

"Hee-lon. Is that how you say it?"

"Yessir," Helon said. "What is your name?"

"Captain Sam Cade," he said. "I am a captain now, but since the war is nearly over, I hope just to be plain Sam Cade before long."

Momma asked him, "Do you think the war is about over?"

"Oh, yes, ma'am. The Confederates are on the run in Virginia. General Sheridan has burned out the Shenandoah Valley, and General Sherman has burned Atlanta and is marching toward Savannah. It won't last six months now. I'm sorry, I didn't mean to sound like you all had been whipped, but I am just so anxious to get this over with and get on home."

Momma said, "I don't know what we will do when the war is over. What we are doing now, I guess. My husband was with the 30th Alabama and fought at Chickamauga and the Cumberland Gap and finally got pneumonia at Vicksburg. He died at Quitman, Mississippi, at a doctor's house. That was in 1863. I wish it had been over before then. I wish we had lost before then. I wish we had surrendered before he died. He should never have gone in the first place. We never had slaves, so I don't know what he went for."

Momma began to cry. Then Helon cried, so I did, too. The Yankee sat in the chair and looked at the fire while we cried. When Momma quit crying, Helon stopped, so I decided I might as well, too.

The soldier turned to me and said, "Jerusha, will you hand me that Bible that I see over on that table?"

I didn't know what to do. I looked at Momma, and she said, "It's all right, Jerusha, go ahead and give it to Mr. Cade."

"Is he going to take it away from us, Momma?" I started crying again. I don't know whether it was because I scared myself with my voice or because I knew the Yankee was going to kill me first now or because I didn't want him to take away anything that my daddy had ever touched.

Momma said, "It's all right. Just hand it to Mr. Cade." So I took him the Bible, but I held it way out from me and didn't get too close in case he grabbed me.

The Yankee took the Bible and opened it and said to Momma, "I always read to my little girls on Christmas Eve. Do you think it would be all right if I read to Jerusha and Helon?"

"I'd like that," Momma said, "and I think they will, too."

So the Yankee took the book and opened it and began to read to us:

> *And she brought forth her first-born son, and wrapped him in swaddling clothes and laid him in a manger, because there was no room for them in the inn.*
>
> *And there were in the same country shepherds abiding in the field, keeping watch over their flock by night.*
>
> *And, lo, the Angel of the Lord came upon them, and the glory of the Lord shone round about them: and they were sore afraid.*
>
> *And the Angel of the Lord said unto them: "Fear not: for, behold, I bring you good tidings of great joy which shall be to all the people.*
>
> *"For unto you is born this day in the city of David a Savior, which is Christ the Lord.*
>
> *"And this shall be a sign unto you. You shall find the babe wrapped in swaddling clothes, lying in a manger."*
>
> *And suddenly there was with the Angel a multitude of the heavenly host praising God and saying, glory to God in the highest and on earth peace, goodwill toward men.*

Momma was crying, so Helon cried. And I cried, too. I don't know why, but we all did. Somehow I found myself standing right by the soldier and he had his hand on my head. It felt good. Then I looked up at Mr. Cade and he was crying, too.

Tommy Earl said after Granny finished the story she sat still for a long time.

"I saw tears in her eyes," he said, "so I started crying, too. I don't know why, but it made me cry to see her cry.

"Granny smiled at me and said, 'That was a long time ago. Way back before I met your granddaddy. Before your daddy was born or your Uncle Henry or your Uncle Grover. I was just a baby, and look at me now. I am an old woman. All that happened, let's see—it's nineteen and thirty-seven now—so that was seventy-three years ago today. But I remember it better than nearly anything that has happened to me since then.'

"She looked off in the distance and said, 'I memorized that part of the Bible that Mr. Cade read to us that night. It's about the only part of the Bible that I can say by heart.'"

Tommy Earl Dell memorized that Bible story and said he would always say it to his children, if he ever had any.

FOUR

"Corinna, Corinna"

1937

The farther north they went, the sadder both of them looked. Grady Dell was driving and Homer Brantley was sitting scrunched up against the passenger side door holding the stump of his arm in his left hand. They hadn't talked since they got on the old, rutted county road 2306 that led them just south of the town of Telephone in Fannin County. They were headed up from Bodark Springs in Eastis County to visit Clint Carter, who had a little run-down farm a few miles south of Telephone.

As they pulled off the road and down the lane that led to Clint's farm, they could see Clint's wife Corine standing on the front porch.

"Uh-oh," Homer said, "she looks mad."

"She always looks mad," Grady said. "I guess staying out here waiting for Clint to die for over a year would make anybody look mad."

"Yeah, but she looks madder than usual. Mad like she might come after us with a butcher knife. I know how she hates it when we show up every month. Just cause we bring Clint a little whiskey to ease him along."

Grady pulled his worn-out Ford up near the front steps and said, "Howdy, Corine."

Corine Carter stood on the top step like a corporal of the guard and said, "I want you two to get your sorry asses out of my yard and out of my life. Now back up that old rattletrap Ford and get out of here or I will go get that twelve-gauge of Clint's and blow the tires off that old wreck. Then you two bastards can walk back to Bodark. Now git!"

Corine was crying as she screamed at the two old World War I veterans. She was not sobbing or choking, but big tears rolled down her cheeks.

"Hey, wait a minute, Corine," Homer said. "We don't mean no harm. We just come to see Clint like we do every month or so. We just—"

"You sorry one-armed son of a bitch, you always come up here sniffing around and slipping whiskey to a dying man. And you, too, Grady Dell. I know you and I know what a sot drunkard you are. I want you gone."

"Well," Grady said, "can we see Clint before we go? Just for a few minutes?"

"Clint ain't here."

"What do you mean 'ain't here'? He ain't been out of that bed in over a year. Where is he at?"

"He's down in Bodark Springs. That's where your sorry asses better head for unless you plan to stop off and get drunk on the way. If you do, I hope you run off in a ditch."

Now Corine Carter was crying hard.

Homer said, "Is he in the hospital or what?"

"He's down there getting embalmed," she sobbed.

Grady almost fell against the front fender of the Ford. He said, "Is Clint dead?"

"No. T. B. Whitmire is just embalming him for the fun of it. Of course he's dead you dumb son of a bitch. Now git off my property."

Grady backed out of the front yard, which hadn't seen a sprig of grass or been swept since Clint got sick. He turned the car's nose back on the road toward Bodark.

They drove for a mile or so before Homer broke the silence: "Old Clint Carter sure took a long time to die. It's a wonder he lived this long. He got shot all to pieces in the Argonne Forest and then you and him took a good bit of that German gas, didn't you?"

"Yeah. Clint and me spent most of the war in the same outfit, but he got shot to hell and I didn't get a scratch. When the gassing started, I got my gas mask on quicker than he did. And then when we took that German machine gun nest, Clint got shot three or four times. He saved my life, too."

"How?"

Grady said, "When we jumped down in that nest one of them Krauts had a bead on me, but Clint saw it in time to ram a bayonet right into his throat. I shot two others but not before Clint got three rounds in his belly. That ended the war for him, but he spent a year or so in the hospital and has been in and out of the VA hospital in Bonham ever since they opened it."

"I don't guess you and Clint got medals for taking out that machine gun nest, did you?"

Grady laughed for the first time since they had been headed back toward Bodark Springs. "Shit, no. I was a PFC and Clint was a buck private. They give medals to officers. That son of a bitch McArthur got the Congressional Medal of Honor for not doing near as much as Clint did. And now McArthur is a hero for running off the bonus marchers in Washington. Son of a bitch turned the tanks on an army of veterans looking for a measly five-hundred-dollar bonus. I guess you got a medal when you got your arm shot off, didn't you?"

"Yeah, I got the Purple Heart. That and a nickel will get you a cup of weak coffee at the Busy Bee Cafe."

They drove in silence for three or four miles and were back across the county line in Eastis County before Homer said, "You was sweet on Corine back before the war, wasn't you?"

"That was before the war. That was before Corine got so damn mean and ugly. I count it a blessing that Clint came back from the war and took her away from me. Even if he hadn't, I would never have taken up with her again. So I guess you can't say he took her away from me, but he always thought he did."

Homer started singing:

> Corinna, Corinna, where you been so long?
> Corinna, Corinna, where you been so long?
>
> Ain't had no lovin since you been gone.

Grady said, "Oh, shut up. You ain't no hand at singing."

Homer said, "I used to see you and her at play parties and box suppers, and you all seemed pretty close, I thought. Did Corine dance back then?"

"Hell no!" Grady said. "Her daddy was old man Sim Pledger, some kind of jackleg Baptist preacher who saw dancing as the worst sin you could do. Next to whiskey, I guess.

"Old man Pledger didn't know that there wasn't much difference between a play party and a dance. They called what passed for dancing as play party games. They sang 'Skip to My Lou' and 'Weevily Wheat' and 'Shoot the Buffalo' and we danced without hugging up."

Homer had to sing again:

> I don't want none of your weevily wheat
> And I don't want your barley,
> Just give me some flour and half an hour
> To bake a cake for Charlie.

Grady decided that Homer's singing wasn't so bad and joined in:

> Take her by her lily white hand
> And lead her like a pigeon,
> Make her dance to "Weevily Wheat"
> Till she loses her religion.

Homer said, "What are we gonna do with the whiskey we brought old Clint? I guess we would empty it out alongside of the road."

Grady said, "I got a half pint of Four Roses so hot in my pocket it might start a brush fire. What did you bring?"

Homer reached under the seat, got his half pint and read laboriously, "Let's see, 'Old Overcoat' it says here. Rye whiskey. Or maybe it's 'Old Overholt.' I can't read the label without my glasses. Anyway, it tastes like an old overcoat, but Clint seemed to like it."

Grady said, "Or we could stop at the Hop Rite Inn and get a couple of chasers to help take the bite out of this cheap whiskey."

Homer said, "You reckon old Peg Leg Watson will let us drink whiskey in his beer joint? Hunh. He lose that leg in the war?"

"No, I think he got it cut off working in Jim Lawrence's sawmill, but he likes for folks to think he was in the war. If he had been in the war, the government would have give him a cork leg and he wouldn't have to stump around on that homemade oak thing with a piece of inner tube nailed to the end."

It was still early in the day, so there were only four cars parked in front of the tarpaper shack that called itself the Hop Rite Inn. It was dark inside, and Grady and Homer slid into one of the back booths. When Ova Jean Watson, old Peg's daughter, came to the booth, she saw Grady and said, "You want the usual?"

Grady said, "Naw, Ova Jean, how about a couple of chasers and maybe a pair of hamburgers to nail down what we plan to drink. If that's all right."

"Okay. Two 7 UPs and two hamburgers. You want them all the way?"

"All the way, heavy on the onions," Homer said.

Once the hamburgers and the 7 UPs were on the table, Homer said, "Now, tell me about when you was sweet on Corine Carter—or Pledger, she was back then. I recollect that she was a right pretty girl back about nineteen and sixteen. But somebody said she was bad to cry over anything. Just like she was crying today when she run us off the place."

Grady remembered the days he courted Corine Pledger. "Oh, she was pretty enough in a plump sort of way, not like the skinny old scarecrow you saw today. But she did cry. Happy or sad, Corine would break into tears. My daddy once said, 'Anybody that cries that much probably never pisses a drop.' But we was never really sweethearts. We took a good many buggy rides and went to some play parties and a few ice cream socials, but I only went with her because there wasn't anybody in my part of Fannin County that I liked."

"And then you came back and married Mamie Earnest."

"No, not directly," Grady said. "I fell in love before I ever got back here. I fell in love in Germany when I was in the Army of Occupation, and didn't get over her for a long time. Maybe I am not really over her today. Every time I hear a certain Lula Bell and Scotty song on the Rock-Ola, I think back to Eva Gerber, the German girl in the house they billeted me in after the Armistice."

Homer said, "I used to wish I could have got in the Army of Occupation. I hear there was frauleins all hot and ready over there after so many Krauts got killed. And beer. I hear that they made a lots better beer than that we can get."

"Well, I never got mixed up with the kind of hot frauleins you are talking about. I moved in with the Gerber family and took to Eva right away. She was promised to somebody else—a man a lot older than she was—but we sure fell in love. Her folks liked me, though we couldn't speak each other's language. But I got a lot of food from the army that they couldn't buy if they had had any money, which they didn't. It was lots of hardtack and bully beef and some fresh meat sometimes. It was the best year of my life. Hell, I don't remember having more than two good years after I was grown."

After they had polished off the Four Roses and a second round of chasers, Homer asked, "When was the other one?"

"The other what?"

"The other good year of your life. Looks to me like you got it pretty good now. You got a job, and that's a lot more than half the people I know have. At least you ain't on the WPA or taking no welfare. And you have got a wife and two kids."

"You ain't married to Mamie, are you?"

"No, I ain't married to nobody. Nobody wants a one-armed man. And when I see how Corine turned out and how hard she was on Clint, I think maybe I was lucky to lose an arm. Better a stump than a wife like Corine."

"Or a wife like Mamie," Grady said, though he never talked against Mamie with most people. But he felt like he and Homer, two old Fannin County vets, had some things in common.

And he said, "She has led me a merry chase. She is always sick, and I am broke from the doctor bills she has run up. I lost the only house I ever owned when I had to borrow six hundred dollars from old Mike Sharp that I couldn't pay back. And Mamie has got a red-hot temper. If she don't get her a shot when she feels like it, there is hell to pay. Old Doc Clayton will give her one, and then she will go to Dr. Elgin for one. And when they think she is getting too many, we have to drive to Sherman where old Doctor Farley, who retired from Bodark Springs, will give her one."

Grady poured some of Homer's Old Overcoat into his half-empty 7 Up and said, "To answer your question: the other good year was when I first got back from Germany. With a broken heart. I stayed out on my daddy's farm for a while and pined for Eva Gerber. Then I took the civil service exam and got on as a rural letter carrier. Used my daddy's old buggy to carry the mail in after I bought old Hobson, the horse I used till I got my first Model T. This was before I met Mamie Earnest and some real warfare began. I took up with old man Mitchell Cogburn's daughter, and for about a year, we had us a high old time."

Homer poured some more of his whiskey into the chaser bottle and said, "She was the girl that got killed in the car wreck over by Savoy, wasn't she?"

"Yeah, her name was Molly. Her and her brother was coming back from Sherman. He was half drunk and pulled out into the railroad crossing just as Number 9 from Texarkana was headed west. Killed both of them outright. So I lost the only two women I loved and found myself married to Mamie about two years later."

"I never knew Mamie. Wasn't she a sister to Shorty Earnest?"

Grady said, "Sort of a half-sister, I guess. Mamie was a bastard, and I think that went a long way to making her the way she is."

"A bastard! What do you mean?"

Grady, by now about two of the allotted three sheets in wind, said, "Yeah. Her momma's husband died and old Ruthie Earnest took in a boarder. That boarder is Mamie's daddy, she thinks. All she knows about him is that his name was Holmes and that he had red hair. Red like Mamie's. Maybe that is what makes her so hot tempered. She blames all her bad luck on being born a bastard."

Homer said, "Didn't I hear that Mamie once shot Shorty in the foot?"

Grady laughed out loud and said, "You heard right. I was off at an American Legion meeting when Shorty and that Bagby boy slipped up to the house hoping to steal the little old owl-head pistol that Mamie's Uncle Isham Earnest left her. We had lost our house in town and was living in a rent house a mile or two out of town. When Shorty didn't see my car and all the lights was out, he and the Bagby boy stood in the road talking about how to get into the house. Mamie heard the talk, and since it was a moonlit night, she could see them standing in the road. So she leaned across Tommy Earl, who was about four at the time, and shot Shorty in the foot. Him and the Bagby boy run down the road, and Shorty's foot got to hurting, so they would stop. Mamie went to the back door, and every time they stopped, she would shoot up in the air. And then they would run some more. And Mamie would shoot when they stopped. She only shot at Shorty the one time, and that didn't wake Tommy Earl, though she shot right across his head out the window screen. I had to get Jimmy Kelly to put me a new screen in."

Homer said, "I saw Shorty in town on crutches back about then. And so Mamie shot him with the gun he meant to steal?"

"No. She shot him with my .32 Savage automatic. I guess since it was a .32, he wasn't crippled for life. Uncle Isham's gun was a .38 Smith and Wesson, and that might have done him a lot more harm."

Homer said, "Maybe you would have been better with Corine after all. If Clint hadn't had such a hard time, she might not have wound up so mean and mad at the world."

"No," Grady said, "I think Corine would have been bitter no matter what. I may not be better off with Mamie, but I wouldn't want to take a chance on Corine. Sometimes Mamie is all right, but then sometimes she gets despondent. One time a year ago, I was out at the American Legion and got home to find a note from her. It said 'I am laying on the railroad tracks. When I am dead, take what of my body is left to the McIlwayne Cemetery and bury it next to my Uncle Isham.'"

"And then what happened?"

Grady said, "We was living in town then, and wasn't more than a quarter of a mile from the tracks, so I run down there and saw her with her head on the tracks. I think she had been laying on the roadbed till she saw me coming. Then she got her head on the tracks. She had taken a pillow with her and she was still adjusting it to her head when I got there. I am pretty sure she just wanted me to see how serious she was about killing herself."

The Hop Rite Inn didn't have many customers since it was the middle of the afternoon on Wednesday. Grady had gotten his substitute, Ross Hurst, to take his route the way he always did when he and Homer went to see Clint. Now it was getting on to four and the whiskey in the Old Overholt bottle was nearly gone. Homer said, "Do you want the last bit of this dead soldier, or should I drain the bottle?"

"You go ahead on," Grady said, "I have to try to drive home, and I'd hate for Chief Orr Starnes or Sheriff Herman Wells to pick me up for drunk driving. But I am like old Jim Nichols, who always says he can drive better drunk than he can sober. I have seen old Jim Nichols drive up in front of the house so drunk he couldn't get out of the car. And then he would drive off just as pretty as you please."

Old Peg Watson stumped over to the booth and said, "You boys gonna sit here all evening on two hamburgers and four 7 UPs? I can't make a living on that kind of money. You could have bought the whiskey off of me instead of getting it from old Tubby Wallace and bringing it into my establishment." He pronounced it "E Stablish Mint."

Homer was on his feet. "I wouldn't hardly call this board and bat tarpaper shack a 'E Stablish Mint.' You only got one leg and I only got one arm, but I am a good mind to whip your ass with that left arm. With that peg leg you look like a pirate in the movies. Did you ever think of getting a cork leg? Your whiskey is made to sell. It ain't made to drank and everybody knows that. That white whiskey you sell has made half the people in Eastis County blind."

Grady hated confrontations, so he said to Homer, "Settle down and let's go on home," and to Peg Watson, "Homer don't mean nothing. We been up to see Clint Carter. We found out he was dead and that's what got Homer in such a bad humor."

Peg Watson—nobody ever knew what his first name was—grunted and stumped off on his homemade leg.

When Grady and Homer got in the Chevrolet, Grady had a hard time finding the keys and a harder time putting the key in the ignition. When he had settled down and cranked up the old car, he said to Homer, "I hope you won't tell anybody all the things I said about Mamie. I suspect it would hurt her feelings."

"Hell," Homer said, "I don't recollect half of what you said. Mixing Four Roses and Old Overcoat may have dulled my head."

Maybe Homer's head had been dulled, or maybe he had just reached that mellow stage that some drunks go through. He said, "Maybe we was too hard on Corine. It must have been hard on her with Clint being so sick for so long."

Grady said, "Old Clint was supposed to be dead a year ago. I guess I ought to be glad he didn't linger any longer. His lungs were shot to hell from the gas. I know how that is because I spend half the night coughing myself. But I am a whole lot better off than Clint. He had bad lungs, a bad heart, and a cancer somewhere inside. I don't know where. He didn't hardly eat, and I bet he weighed less than a hundred pounds the last time we saw him."

Grady said, "I am glad we bought him pretty good bonded whiskey when we come up here to see him. But the shape he was in, he'd have drunk furniture polish. I know how Corine hated whiskey, but she tolerated us slipping him a little. Mamie and Corine was both raised brush arbor Baptist and begrudged a fellow a little nip. Either one of them could smell a drank of whiskey over the telephone."

Homer said, "You know if Clint and Corine had had children, she might have an easier time of it. I wonder why they didn't."

Grady said, "I know the answer to that. Clint got the mumps when we was at St. Mihiel and they fell on him."

"What do you mean 'they fell on him'?"

Grady said, "If you get the mumps and you can't go to bed right away, they will fall down into your balls. Hell, we was in the middle of battle and Clint had to keep going. His balls swelled up as big as baseballs. After the war, the doctor told him he could never have children."

"I guess we was way too hard on Corine after all she's been through, but she could have been a little friendlier when we drove up at her house today."

Grady said, "I guess so, but I think maybe if she had had half a chance in her life, she might not have turned out so hard. Poor old thing. I remember her when she was a girl, and way back then, I felt sorry for her."

Homer said, for the second time, "I may have been lucky that gals wouldn't take to a one-armed man. I might have got myself into some kind of mare's nest with a woman that would have made my life hell."

"Oh, come on Homer. I've seen that fat girl of Lige Attaway's making eyes at you."

"I might rather be laying a corpse in old T. B. Whitmire's

funeral parlor than married to that old cross-eyed fat girl."

Grady loved ragging Homer, "But she sure seems sweet on you, and she might be so glad to get a man that she would treat you right. But hell, she makes eyes at every man who passes by. I can't hardly stop to deliver old Lige's mail that she don't come out and try to get me to eat something she has cooked. Once she wanted me to cure her warts. But I told her I had forgot how."

"Oh, yeah, that's right! You used to cure warts all over the county. How did you do it?"

"I can't tell you or I would lose the gift. I'll tell you what I did, though. I would get an old gal to count her warts and tell me how many she had, and then I would rub my hand over them. And before long they would disappear."

"What if the warts was in some private place? Did you rub, you know, down there?"

"That's the part I can't tell you about, Homer. If I did, you might die or get took with some bad disease."

Homer said, "I damn sure don't want no curse put on me, so don't tell me any more. Did you get that gift in Germany after the war?"

"No, I got it from my daddy, but I used it a time or two in Germany after the war." Grady laughed and sighed at that memory.

They drove on a ways and Grady said, "I guess I shouldn't bellyache too much about my life. My kids are working out all right and I have a government job here in the middle of this Depression. But goddamn it, it's always something. Mamie who drives me broke with doctor's bills for stuff that Doctor Clayton says is all in her head. And then there is that damn Melvin Spruille. Melvin is a son of a bitch to work for. Jack Hurst, the Republican postmaster, wasn't bad, but damn Melvin will make you want to take a drank of whiskey every time you hear his grating voice."

Grady said, "I still have my two fox hounds and go huntin' every week or two. I bought my two fox hounds—a July and a Walker—off of old Doc Bates and took to fox hunting after I got back from the war and before I met Mamie."

"Did you ride a horse and chase after the dogs? That's how they did it in a book I read when I was in that hospital in England."

"No," Grady said, "we call it 'still hunting.' You get a bunch of old boys and several pints of whiskey and take your dogs out in the woods and set 'em loose. Then you build a fire and let the dogs run, hoping they hit a fox's trail."

"And then what?"

"Then nothing. You sit and listen to them run the fox. You build up a fire and drink a little whiskey. Old Doc Bates says he had rather hear dogs on the chase than listen to a brass band. Old Doc has that Model B Ford all painted up saying 'Blue Ribbon Shoe Shop' and under it 'Texas's Greatest Foxhunter.' After the dogs find a fox and run it, you blow on your horn and call 'em back. I got my brother Henry to make me a horn after he had to kill an old cow he had. He just hollered it out and smoothed off the blowing end to fit your mouth."

Homer, who had never hunted anything, said, "Then the dogs come back when you blow that horn?"

"Not always. I have spent many a Sunday morning driving all over Eastis County and half of Fannin calling up my dogs. But they always get hungry and come to the sound of the horn."

"That don't sound like a lot of fun to me," Homer said.

"Well, it beats going to church. That's where I'd be if I had married Corine. Every Sunday hearing her daddy preach hellfire and damnation and brimstone and what not and the like."

They drove on for a mile or two and then Homer began to sing in his middling tenor voice:

Corinna, Corinna, where'd you sleep last night?

Corinna, Corinna, where'd you sleep last night?
You come in this morning when the sun got bright.

Grady couldn't help himself and helped Homer with the old song:

I met Corinna far across the sea.
I met Corinna far across the sea.
She didn't write me no letter,
She didn't care for me.
Corinna, Corinna.
I love Corinna, tell the world I do,
I love Corinna, tell the world I do.
I just wish she would love me too.

Homer and Grady were still singing as they made it to the outskirts of Bodark Springs.

With two moons rising.

FIVE

The Return of Jesse James

1938

"Grady! Hey, Grady, hold up a minute!"

Grady Dell, the rural letter carrier, was trying to balance his mail sack on the hood of his brand-new 1938 Chevrolet while he pulled the undelivered parcel post out of the passenger side.

Tall, skinny Tarp Davidson, the Bodark Springs walking mailman, was hurrying toward Grady with his mailbag flopping against his side, his head jerking back and forth, and the biggest Adam's apple in Eastis County bobbing up and down.

The day was over for both Grady and Tarp, and Tarp was in a good mood. Grady wasn't. He couldn't wait to get checked up and out of the post office so he could run by bootlegger Tubby Wallace's trailer house and get him a drink of whiskey or two on the way home.

Grady knew all Tarp's tricks and knew he had a piece of gossip that he couldn't wait to make Grady drag out of him.

"Dang, Grady, I ain't never seen a new car that dirty. How long you had it? What's it been now—a week?"

"Might near two weeks. Mamie and Jackie have washed it three times already, but that road up near Ivanhoe is a loblolly this time of year. I got stuck up there today and had to get old man Will Scoggins to pull me out with them two old blue mules of his. But, hell, it drives just as good dirty as it does clean."

Tarp said, "You better tell Mamie that; ain't no use in telling me. Say, if you had got in on time today, you wouldn't have missed the fight over by the courthouse." Tarp started laughing.

Grady figured Tarp had a joke ready, but he said, "I'll bite, who's been fightin'?"

"Naw, this ain't no joke. It was Lark and Hammaker that had a fight."

Grady laughed, "Yeah? I'll bet. Hell, Lark and Hammaker must be ninety years old."

"Ninety-one."

"Well, whatever they are, they're damn sure too old to fight."

"Not today, they wasn't," Tarp said. "They got into it over Jesse James."

"Jesse James? Hell, Lark and Hammaker never rode with Jesse James. Lark may have bought a suit from Frank James back in the teens, when Frank was working at E. M. Kahn's store in Dallas. But I know Hammaker didn't buy nothing from Frank. He never had a suit in his life."

"They didn't fight over the real Jesse James. They got to arguing about that feller that's going around claiming to be Jesse. You know, the one that is coming to the Pines Theater next week."

Grady was puzzled. He said, "I don't know about nobody coming to the Pines next week. What is it, a picture show?"

"Picture show nothing! This is the real thing. Didn't you see that big ad that Harry Willoughby run in the paper that come out last night?"

Grady balanced his sack and packages and moved toward the back door of the post office as Tarp got out his key and let them in. Grady turned to Tarp once they had put their sacks down and said, "I didn't see this week's paper. I guess ours didn't come last night. Or maybe Mamie used it to wrap something up in. At our house you never can tell. If there is something about the high school in the paper, Jackie cuts it out for her scrapbook. If she don't, Tommy Earl is likely to turn the front two pages into a kite before I get to read it. What did the paper say about Jesse James?"

Tarp, as chinless as Andy Gump in the funny papers, cackled and snorted and said, "Hell, Old Harry has found some old drunk about a hundred years old to come and get up on the stage and claim he's Jesse James and that he didn't get killed back whenever it was and has been hidin' out ever since the Civil War. Now Harry claims this old man's touring the country and telling the real story of how he robbed from the rich and give it to the poor—or kept it hisself most likely. And Old Lark Bagwell fell for it—hook, line, and sinker. But Hammaker, he says Lark's a fool for believing anything Harry Willoughby says. Hammaker says Lark is going soft and is going to get all his money stole if he keeps on believing every crook that comes through Eastis County."

Grady turned his mail sack upside down on his desk to get out everything that had to be bundled and put on Number 32 for Texarkana at 5:46. As he sorted the mail, he asked Tarp, "Has Lark got any money for anybody to steal?"

Tarp said he didn't know but he guessed maybe Lark still owned land out north of Windom in Fannin County where he and Hammaker had grown up. Then Tarp launched into the life stories of Lark and Hammaker. "You knowed," Tarp said, "that Lark and Hammaker growed up together and went off to fight in the Civil War together when they was just shirt-tail boys, didn't you? You knowed they farmed side by side out there till they got too old. You knowed, I reckon, that they moved into Bodark when they got to be about seventy—back about when you got drafted into the army and went across the water to fight the Kaiser. You knowed all that didn't you, Grady?"

Grady kept sorting his mail for tomorrow as Tarp kept narrating the biographies of Lark and Hammaker. Grady kept his back turned toward Tarp until Tarp had run down. Then he turned and said, "Of course I know all that stuff. I was raised on the farm next to Lark's. I know both of them a whole lot better than you do. And I know Lark Bagwell ain't a fool. If he thinks this feller could be Jesse, he may have a reason."

"A reason? A reason? Well, hell, Grady, you don't think Jesse James is still alive, too, do you?"

Grady said he didn't know anything about it. Then he thought awhile and added, "Ain't it against the law to advertise that somebody is somebody he ain't? I mean, can Harry Willoughby just say that Jesse James is coming and then get some old drunk to come in and say he is Jesse? How old is Jesse James now?"

"Grady, Jesse James is dead. He ain't no old. But if he was still alive, he would be ninety-one—the same age as Lark and Hammaker."

Grady stared at Tarp and thought. Then he grinned and said, "How do you know it ain't Jesse?"

"Aw, hell, Grady, not you, too. Don't you start in about Jesse still being alive and coming to Bodark Springs, Texas. Shit, this is 1938, and they don't have fairy tales no more. I'm telling you Jesse James is dead and buried. Didn't you ever hear the song that Ross and Kate Hurst used to sing about how Jesse was betrayed by some feller named Ford when Jesse was disguised as a man named Howard and how Ford shot Jesse in the back?"

"I may have—I don't remember."

Tarp tried to sing a little of the song, but he couldn't get the tune right, so he recited the refrain for Grady—and for Melvin Spruille, the postmaster, who had closed the post office windows and was waiting to check Grady and Tarp out before adding up his own cash box. Tarp said in a singsong,

> That dirty little coward
> That shot Mister Howard,
> And laid pore Jesse in his grave.

"Didn't you never hear that? How about you, Melvin?"

Grady said he hadn't, but Melvin thought he might have heard Ross Hurst sing something like that. He couldn't be sure.

Tarp, exasperated at Grady for believing that Jesse might still be alive, said to Melvin, "Well at least you don't believe that Jesse James is alive and is coming to the Pines Theater next week."

Melvin, who hadn't thought much about it, decided to side with Grady against Tarp. He said, "Well, I guess Grady might be right. I don't suppose Harry Willoughby would claim somebody was Jesse James if he wasn't."

Tarp turned back to his desk and started scrabbling around in his incoming mail and mumbling, "I never will understand how two grown men . . ."

Tarp was still muttering as Grady and Melvin went to the front so Grady could turn in his COD money and what he had collected for money orders and stamps. Melvin was grinning when he said to Grady, "I see Tarp told you about Lark Bagwell and John Hammaker scuffling around up on the square."

Grady laughed, "Yeah. He told me. I wasn't sure whether to believe him until he got mad because I wouldn't agree that Jesse James was dead."

Melvin said, "You think Jesse might still be alive?"

"No," Grady said, "I doubt it, but I like to get away with old Tarp every once in a while." He said this under his breath so Tarp wouldn't hear. Then he asked Melvin about the fight.

"Aw, it wasn't no fight. Lark and Hammaker got to arguing. Then they fell in to cussing, and Lark pushed Hammaker off the end of the bench. Hammaker come up swinging, but nobody got hurt. Hell, them old boys is ninety years old."

"Ninety-one," Tarp hollered from his desk.

Grady was still laughing at Tarp for fuming over Jesse James as he left the post office and walked across to the courthouse to see if the two old men were still at it. He didn't see anybody on the benches and began to worry that the two old Civil War veterans had really had a serious falling out. He decided that he would stop off in the morning before he left on his route and see if they had made it up.

On the way home, Grady stopped by Tubby Wallace's trailer house and had two water glasses half full of Four Roses whiskey to put him in a mood to go home. Then he had one more drink to the memory of Jesse James, who was, his Momma always claimed, a distant relative.

At home that night, Mamie and Jackie and Tommy Earl were all talking non-stop about Jesse James coming to town next week. Mamie and Jackie said they didn't plan to go see a criminal and a murderer and that Harry Willoughby ought to be shut down for putting on such as that. Tommy Earl begged Grady to take him to see the famous outlaw that had a poem about him. Tommy Earl said that his teacher, Evelyn Bailey, had read the poem to the class at school in honor of Jesse's visit to Bodark Springs. Tommy Earl borrowed the book during study hall and wrote down some of the verses.

"Daddy, let me read you that poem about Jesse," Tommy Earl said as he ran to get his book satchel.

Grady called to the boy, "Son, you know I ain't no hand for poetry. I don't know that I would underst—"

"Grady," Mamie said in a stage whisper, "You know what Evelyn said about helping him with his studies. Let him read it, you hear?"

"All right. Okay. I'll listen, but I still may not understa—"

Tommy Earl cut Grady off with, "Okay, here goes." And in a seven-year-old's singsong he read,

> Crack, crack, crack, and the street ran flames
> And a great voice bellowed, "I'm Jesse James."

"And here's another part:

> He swayed through the coaches with horns and a tail
> Lit out with the bullion and the registered mail.

"And, wait, this here's how it ends:

> They're creeping, they're crawling, they're stalking/ Jess,
> Roll on Missouri
> But the son of a gun's gone farther West
> Brown Missouri, roll.

"How do you like that, Daddy?"

"That's not bad. Not bad a-tall. What's that part about 'Roll on Missouri' mean?"

Tommy Earl was as puzzled as Grady was about Benet's refrain, but since he had read the poem in the first place he felt compelled to answer something, so he said, "It's just a part of the poem. They all have stuff like that in them."

Grady, remembering his school days, and remembering a poem that had a puzzling "nevermore" about every three lines, said, "Yeah, I guess that's right. And I guess that's why I never was no hand at poems."

As the evening wore on and Grady wore down, he promised to take Tommy Earl to see Jesse James when—if—the famous outlaw showed up at the theater.

The next morning Grady drove around by the courthouse on his way out of town to carry the mail. He saw Lark and Hammaker sitting side by side on their bench as they had been doing for better than twenty years. He stopped and got out and walked over to where they sat. He supposed that the fight had been settled, and he didn't mean to bring it up, so he said, "Howdy, boys. Thought I would stop and see if Lark had any messages for Earlene. I have to stop by her house on the route today to give her some change for a money order I sold her yestiddy. You got any messages, Lark?"

"No, much obliged, Grady, but I'll see her next week when she comes to town to see Jesse James," Lark said in the calmest of voices.

Hammaker smiled at Grady and said, "How's your folks, Grady?"

"Fine, Mr. Hammaker, just fine. Momma's nearly got over that stroke of paralysis she had last winter. How about you? You all right?"

Hammacher looked thoughtful and said, "I'm fine, Grady. I couldn't be better. I've got my health, and my mind is as sound as a silver dollar." He stood up and looked off toward the cottonseed mill across the T&P tracks and said, "You know, Grady, me and Lark Bagwell here growed up next to each other out there beside your daddy's farm. I knowed your daddy all his life. And I've knowed you all yours. Ain't that right? Now, ain't it?"

"Yessir, yessir, that's a fact. Except for some of my family, I guess I have known you and Lark longer than I have anybody else in the world."

For some reason everybody—children and grown people—called Bagwell "Lark"; in fact, half the people in Bodark Springs didn't know what his last name was. Hammaker was always called "Hammaker" or "Mr. Hammaker." Even Grady didn't know his first name. Hammaker had never married, and since the death of Lark's wife in 1893—of pneumonia—the two old men had been inseparable. Lark lived with his son Charley, a retired railroad man, and Hammaker lived in a little house that he and Lark had built in Charley's backyard.

Hammaker kept looking at Grady and said, in the same matter-of-fact voice, "Me and Lark growed up out north of Windom. When we was sixteen—in eighteen and sixty-three—we joined the Confederate army. We fought under Hood and we surrendered with General Lee at Appomattox courthouse. And then we walked home together. Walked ever step of the way. Side by side."

Lark looked down at the ground between his feet, and Grady thought he saw tears in his eyes. Grady felt that tightening in his throat that came to men who couldn't cry. Hammaker paused and drew in his breath and went on, "And, Grady, I never knowed that I was a-walking back to Texas with a God-damned fool."

Lark was up in a flash, "You reprobated son of a bitch! You calling me a fool?"

Lark lunged at Hammaker and threw a haymaker at his head. Grady had stepped between them just in time to catch Lark's fist behind the ear. He thought he had been kicked by a mule.

"God dammit, boys, that'll do!"

Hammaker and Grady and Lark all turned to see Herman Wells, the sheriff of Eastis County, standing not three feet away with his hands on his hips.

He motioned to Grady with his head to step aside, and then he said to Lark and Hammaker, "Boys, there ain't nobody in this county that I respect more than I do you all. You all's people was some of the first people to come into this part of Texas. And you two men fought in the war. And was heroes. I've looked up to you all all my life. But if I hear one more goddamned word about this Jesse James business—or I hear anybody else tell me that you two have been fighting about this—I'll lock both of you up in the county jail till that damned bankrobber, or whatever he is, is out of Bodark."

Wells turned to walk away, and then he turned back, "And I may put Harry Willoughby and this damned Jesse James in the same cell with you two. Hell, you boys are ninety years old and ought to know better than to fight."

He turned away for good and headed back toward the basement of the courthouse.

"Ninety-one," Lark and Hammaker said in unison.

Grady and Tommy Earl got to the Pines Theater at six thirty and were among the last customers to get a seat. They were way in the back, but they could see Lark and Hammaker on the front row.

Tommy Earl said, "What time do you reckon Lark and Mr. Hammaker had to get here to get them seats down in the front?"

"Probably spent the night here," Grady said. "Or maybe they had Harry rope off them seats for 'em. Probably threatened to whip him. I don't know about Hammaker, but old Lark hits about as good a lick as I ever felt." Grady still had a knot over his ear.

At seven o'clock, Harry Willoughby came on stage and announced that there would be three shows tonight instead of two. Since the house was already full, he was going to ask everyone to be quiet and to bring on with a great round of applause one of the great heroes of America, "that great train robber and two-gun man, Jesse James!"

The audience went wild as Harry went off stage left.

From the right of the stage came a frail old man in a brown suit with a long-tailed coat. His hair was painfully thin and white and was parted down the middle. But what showed most on his head was the brownness of his scalp. It was almost as muddy brown as the suit he wore.

He sat down on a straight chair in the middle of the stage,

and Harry Willoughby brought a microphone out and put it off to one side. The old man began telling the real story about how he, Robert Ford, Frank, and some of the other boys had made it up for Ford to pretend to kill Jesse and how they buried a coffin full of rocks and how it was raining and how he, Jesse, stood off in the distance, all covered up in a rain cape and hat, and watched his own funeral. He told about hiding out in Arizona for all these years, and how, now that the heat was off him, he was going across America telling his story to the people.

Suddenly a commotion broke out in the front of the theater. Everybody was on his feet, so Grady couldn't see what was happening, but he heard Hammaker's deep bass voice say, "You reprobated son of a bitch!"

Then he heard Earlene Mitchell scream, "You can't call my daddy no son of a bitch!"

From the grunts and groans, he knew somebody was scuffling. He heard Lark say, "You get up, you old bastard, and I'll knock you down again."

Suddenly the old man on the stage was on his feet leaning over the apron of the stage, and two .36 Navy Colts appeared by magic out from under his armpits.

"Set!" It was more of a croak than a shout, but instantly there was not a sound in the theater.

"I said set down!"

Everybody sat.

He walked over in front of Lark and Hammaker and pointed the two guns right at them, "You old men could have rode with me and Frank, and I don't want to have to kill you, but I aim to tell my story. Do you hear? And I don't aim to be interrupted by nobody. Do you hear?" The theater was dead quiet.

"Do you men hear me?"

Lark spoke up and said, "Yes, Jesse."

Hammaker stood silent. He looked far off into the distance.

Maybe he could see all the way back to the Shenandoah Valley. He seemed strangely bemused.

The old man on the stage waved the left-hand gun back and forth about half an inch each way and said to Hammaker, "Do you hear me?"

Hammaker took his time. He looked at Lark and he looked at the old man and he said, "I hear you, Jesse."

The old man said, "You boys in the war?"

They nodded yes, and the old man said, "Hell, I'm glad you boys are still fightin'. You must be ninety."

"Ninety-one!" the audience shouted in unison and then broke up in laughter.

Nobody in Bodark Springs ever knew for sure whether the old man on the stage was Jesse James. All anybody learned from Herman Wells was that the .36 Navy Colts didn't have caps, balls, or firing pins. The argument about whether the old man was really Jesse raged all through May and June. The man claiming he was Jesse James appeared in theaters all along State Highway 5 that cut through Clarksville, Bodark Springs, Paris, and Bonham. He had already been in Clarksville and Paris before coming to Bodark Springs. Then he went on to Bonham and Sherman. The last mention of him in the Bodark Springs *Democrat* was when his appearance provoked a big outcry in Gainesville. Then all the speculation died down. But it might have gone on all summer if Jesus hadn't come to town.

Grady, of course, heard about the Lord's visit from Tarp. "You know Edna Earle Morris, don't you? That lives down on Star Street not far from the cotton mill? The one that married that sorry Morris boy from out at Savoy? Roy Gene Morris. You know, you once called Edna Earle the prettiest girl in Bodark Springs?"

Grady grinned, remembering the times he had driven out of his way to go down Star Street just to see her sitting on her front porch. He remembered for thirty seconds and then said, "Naw, I never said she was the prettiest girl in Bodark."

"The hell you didn't. I was standing right here when—"

Grady laughed and said, "You don't remember too good, Tarp; I said she was the prettiest woman in Eastis County. She ain't too smart, the way I hear it, but Lord have mercy she is pretty. Why? You been carrying night mail out that way?"

Tarp laughed, "No, but I have studied about it. Well anyway, here is the story on her as I get it. Last Thursday she was standing in her kitchen ironing. Wasn't wearing nothing but a slip. You remember how hot it was Thursday?"

Grady was impatient, "Yeah, yeah, I remember how hot it was. It's always hot in July. And it must be hottern' hell in them little old shotgun houses down on Star Street. What about her standing there in her slip? Did you see her?"

"Naw, I didn't see her, but I wish I would have. Anyway, quit interrupting and listen. She was standing there ironing,"—"arning," he pronounced it—"wasn't wearing nothing but a slip. Had the screen door latched. And she says Jesus Christ walked into the kitchen, right through that screen door and sat down at her kitchen table and said to her, 'Edna Earle, I am your Lord and Savior, Jesus Christ, and I have come because I want you to help me bring this den of iniquity back to me and my Heavenly Father.'"

Grady interrupted Tarp, "What den of iniquity? If he was talking about Bodark, it ain't gonna be much of a job. You damn Baptists have got it so dry you can't get a drink of whiskey without driving up nearly to the Red River or over into Fannin County—unless you know where Tubby Wallace's trailer house is at. Now if he's talking about the north part of the county, it's gonna take more than him and Edna Earle to bring them cusses back to the Lord."

Tarp didn't like his stories interrupted, so he just stood and sucked at this teeth until Grady had finished. "As I was saying, Edna Earle said Jesus was wearing a long white robe and except for having a beard and long hair, he looked just like Wayne

Morris."

"Who?"

Tarp grinned, not answering right away, milking his story. Now he was ready to let Grady talk—as long as Grady asked him the right questions.

Grady said, "Well?"

Tarp waited and grinned.

Grady said, "I done asked you once. Now tell me. Who in the hell is Wayne Morris? Is he one of them triflin' damn Morrises from down around Leonard? One of that old Hawk Morris's boys?"

"Naw, you know, the movie star that was in *Kid Galahad*, that boxing movie that was down at the Pines Theater just after Jesse James was."

Grady threw his mail into his sack and said, "Jesus Christ. If all this damn foolishness keeps up, I think I'm gonna move to Paris. Or Sherman. Hell, maybe even to Fort Worth." And he walked out to his new 1938 Chevrolet Standard that already had 1,200 miles on it and drove off to carry the route that he had been running since 1919.

SIX

The Pink Petticoat

1 9 3 8

At six thirty on a cold, blue, drizzling East Texas Monday morning, Grady Dell pulled into his parking space beside the Bodark Springs Post Office. He wanted to be early so Melvin Spruille, the postmaster, and Charlie Stone, the window clerk, would be so busy working the weekend mail that they wouldn't have any time to notice how hung over he was. Charlie was a deacon in the Primitive Baptist Church, and Melvin preached every third Sunday at the Baptist Church over in Dodd City in Fannin County. They both hated whiskey. They also hated other people's sin.

Grady hoped to get his weekend mail sorted so he could run across the square to the Busy Bee Cafe for a quick cup of coffee and a piece of dry toast before the morning mail came in on Number 31. Grady had his mail sorted and sacked and was headed out the side door when Melvin called to him, "You might as well take your time, Grady. Number 31 is going to be an hour late according to Max over at the T&P. Maybe you ought to try eating a little something."

"Yeah, I guess I might as well."

Damn, Grady thought, I hoped he wouldn't notice. If my job wasn't civil service, Melvin would've got rid of me the day Hoover left office and Melvin took over as postmaster from Jack Hurst. Not a single one of them Spruilles ever took a drink. I guess that's what makes 'em so damned mean. I guess I could stay as sober as Melvin and Charlie if I didn't need a little something to steady my nerves once in a while. I'd probably be a heap better off if I didn't, but hell, I might wind up as sour as old Melvin. Damn, if Franklin D. runs for a third term in 1940, I may be working for Melvin till I retire.

Grady held Friday's copy of the *Dallas Morning News* over his head as he crossed the square to the Busy Bee. He tried to see who was inside, but the windows were all fogged, so he squared his shoulders, opened the door, and went in. He walked the length of the counter to sit on the end stool and be away from the early regulars up at the front. He nodded and spoke to six or seven people, but kept moving to avoid small talk.

He sat on the last stool in front of the window that opened into the kitchen and nodded to Modell Floyd, the cook. Modell grinned and said, "How you, Mr. Grady?"

"Fine, Modell, how's your momma?"

"She about to get well. Dr. Clayton first said she gonna have to have that gall bladder took out. But Momma say she ain't lettin' nobody at her with a knife without he slip up on her. Then Dr. Clayton decide Momma just have some kind of infection. She gonna be fine, I guess. How Miss Mamie? She still sick all the time?"

"Most of the time. If it ain't one thing, it's another."

Modell sighed, "Yeah, it be that way sometime."

Bernice Mayes, the waitress, slid a cup of coffee in front of Grady and said, "You look like you could use some of this. Want anything to eat?"

"I guess so. You reckon you got anything I can keep down?" Grady had known Bernice a long time—some people even thought he might know her a little better than he was supposed to.

Bernice looked sympathetic and said, "I'll have Modell scramble you a couple of hen eggs and fix you a slice of dry toast." She turned around and gave the order to Modell. Then she leaned over the counter toward Grady and said, "You feel as bad as you look?"

Grady, with a Lucky Strike in one hand and his chin cupped in the other, said, "I don't know how bad I look, Bernice, but I'd have to get better to die."

Bernice laughed, but she kept it low so as not to add a jolt to Grady's throbbing head. "You looked like you felt good Saturday night when I seen you and Mamie up at the Briar Patch. I thought Mamie had sick headaches all the time, but you and her was dancing every dance."

Grady gave a weak grin and said, "She usually gets well on the weekend—and during the week if I mention going up to the Briar Patch or somewhere."

Bernice looked disgusted at the thought of Mamie's famous illnesses and said, "You must mention honky-tonking a good deal. I see you all every time I go out."

"Well, it's better to go out than to stay home and have to call the doctor. 'Course sometimes she gets sick when we get in, and then I have to walk over to Cooter Poe's house and wake them up and call old Clayton. You know how he cusses when you call him late, but he usually comes out and gives her a shot."

"Mamie don't drink, does she?"

"Oh, Lord, no! Mamie can smell a shot of whiskey over the telephone. She says she hates for me to take a drink, but she'll put up with it to get to go honky-tonking. Maybe that's why I'm always ready to go up to the Red River as soon as it gets dark."

Bernice blushed and lowered her voice, "You ever think about going by yourself? Or maybe taking somebody else?"

"I guess I've thought about it, but somehow it never works out that way."

Bernice hesitated till she got her nerve up. Then she blurted it out in a hoarse whisper, "Did you ever think about coming by my house when you get off from work? Like maybe today about four thirty? You might could use a drink of that Four Roses that Burl Weems left at my house last week. I'll even give you some ice and a Co-Cola to go with it. I may even have some 7 UP."

She didn't wait for Grady to answer but kept talking, getting redder the more she said. "Old Charley Fite calls 7 UP 'a chaser.' Did you know that? When he comes in here to order one, he never says, 'Bernice, give me a 7 UP'; he always says, 'Bernice, give me a chaser.' Old Charlie always—"

Grady held up his hand to cut her off. And then he whispered, "I've thought about coming by a lot, but I don't know. Somehow, it don't seem right. I don't know. I guess as small as Bodark Springs is—"

Bernice was suddenly furious, "Hell, don't nothing seem right. Not a damned thing. Not anymore. They say they are gonna have another war and that that crazy damned Hitler is gonna take over the world. That damned Roosevelt says the Depression is over, but I ain't seen no sign of it. All I see is that I am working my ass off in this damned cafe and—"

Grady was halfway off the stool and was shaking his hand back and forth in front of him trying to get Bernice to quieten down. "Hush, Bernice, everybody in here can hear you. You know how they talk in a town like this."

Bernice lowered her voice, but she didn't end her litany. "The whole damned world is crazy. Remember this spring—when was it, May?—when that old man claiming he was Jesse James come to town to the Pines Theater and nearly caused

Lark and Hammaker to fall out for good? And in the summer that fool Edna Earle Morris claimed that Jesus Christ his own self just waltzed into her house one evening about three o'clock, come right through a locked screen door where she was ironing. And her not wearing nothing but a pink petticoat. And Jesus started telling her some crap about how him and her was going to save Bodark from sin. I mean, can you believe that fool girl? And can you believe that half the people in Eastis County thought she was telling the truth? And now that damned hussy is missing." Bernice put her hands on her hips and turned away; then she wheeled back toward Grady and said—loud this time—"And now you are worried because somebody might see you. And what about me? What if somebody sees me? Nobody gives a damn if somebody sees me. I don't give a shit—"

Bernice sobbed and ran out through the kitchen.

Bear Higgins, the owner of the Busy Bee, came down the counter toward Grady. Bear never smiled and hardly ever spoke. Mostly he just grunted at his customers. He approached Grady looking even sourer than usual and said, "What in the hell did you do to Bernice?"

"Nothing."

"Then why in the hell did she fall in to crying and run out of here? Did you say something out of the way to her?"

Grady, usually one of the best-humored men in the county, suddenly felt a fury come over him. He half rose from the stool and gritted his teeth at Bear Higgins, "Did you ever hear me say anything out of the way to her or any other woman? Well, did you? Hell no, you never did. And I didn't say nothing to Bernice. Now, am I going to get anything to eat in this goddamned cafe or not?"

Grady's headache pounded so much that his anger drained away instantly and he sat back on the stool. Bear, apparently satisfied, didn't speak but turned and lumbered back to the front of the cafe. Modell, seeing and hearing everything, waited till Bear was back at the cash register; then she came out the swinging door from the kitchen bringing Grady's eggs and toast in one hand and a glass of tomato juice in the other.

"Here, Mr. Grady, drink this and eat them eggs and you may make it till dinner. But I'll tell you this, if you don't eat something, you may plumb shake yourself to death." She laughed silently and turned to the urn to get him another cup of coffee.

"Thank you, Modell, I'm much obliged."

"Aw, it ain't nothing, Mr. Grady."

Everybody in Eastis County knew Grady Dell—and liked him. He was always polite, and he never grumbled when people on his route asked him to bring them something from Bodark—a few groceries, medicine from the drugstore, even a few yards of cloth from H. Goldberg's Department Store. All Grady asked was that the women on his route send a note telling Harry Goldberg exactly what kind of yard goods they wanted and what color. Every day the mail ran, Grady delivered two nickel packages of Speedo Headache Powders to Warsaw Bryant's wife. If she didn't have a dime, Grady took her the powders anyway. Warsaw was serving a year and a day in prison for making bootleg whiskey, and Grady figured that Ola May Bryant had a good reason to have a headache. Most people in town knew that Grady had been drinking for the past five or six years, but they put it down to his having to take a mortgage on the house when he couldn't pay Mamie's doctor bills, and then losing the house when he couldn't make the payments. And then there was Mamie's sickness, which Dr. Clayton said was all in her head. Grady never complained to Mamie about being sick, and he never failed to call the doctor when she had one of her "jumping headaches" in the middle of the night. Lindley Spruille at the drugstore once told Grady, "You are getting 'most too many prescriptions for Dilaudid filled," so Grady started getting some filled at Spruille's and some at Doc Miller's. But he knew he wasn't fooling either Lindley or Doc Miller. He thought, I'd rather have a tooth pulled than go into either one of them damn drugstores with a prescription in my hand, but he never complained to Mamie. It wouldn't have done any good, because Mamie complained enough for both of them. She always had a lot to say about his drinking. He always said the same thing back to her, "I could quit if I wanted to. I just drink a little something ever once in a while to settle my nerves." And he thought that was all it amounted to.

Grady nursed his hangover and waited to hear Number 31 blow its whistle. He ate the eggs and toast that Modell brought him and thought he might keep the food down after all. By the time he had finished eating, Bernice had come back from outside looking as if she had never shed a tear in her life. She went up and down the counter pouring coffee and joking with the customers. Maybe Modell's breakfast had saved his life, Grady thought. He lit his eighth Lucky Strike cigarette of the day as Tarp Davidson came in the front door.

Tarp, the city mail carrier, loved carrying the mail. It was pure fun for Tarp to walk all over Bodark and go in all the stores with the day's mail. He stopped to visit people sitting out on their porches, and if nobody was sitting out, Tarp took his pleasure in reading people's postcards as he walked along between houses. When Buck Lawson wrote cards home to his folks from Idaho where he was in the CCC camp, he always wrote at the bottom, "Hello Tarp!" Estelle Lawrence, who was always out in her yard working in her flower bed or feeding her chickens or sweeping the yard when Tarp came by, got most of her mail read to her. Tarp would open the gate and walk up the walk, and, while Mrs. Lawrence was wiping off her hands on her apron to take her letters, he would announce the news from her daughter in Dallas. "Well, let's see. You got a card here from Inez. Says she likes her new job. Says she may be coming home week after next." Tarp didn't seem to worry about the privacy guaranteed by the US mail. Tarp thought if you had a secret you didn't want told, you ought to put it in a letter and not on a penny postcard.

He was all smiles as he came down the counter, nodding and speaking and pausing to dispense a bit of gossip here or a wisecrack there. When he got to the end of the counter, he slid onto the stool and said, "Hidy, Grady, you gonna live after all? Melvin said we might have to bury you."

Grady winced, "I guess I'm good for another day. I hate it that old Melvin noticed I was hung over."

Tarp could hardly wait to pass beyond pleasantries and get to the real news, so he just made a pouring motion in Bernice's direction and said to Grady, "Well, I guess you heard that Edna Earle Morris is missing?" Without waiting for a reply, Tarp began whispering his version of her disappearance.

About three months before, Edna Earle had had a visit from Jesus. The way Tarp told the story, she was standing in the kitchen of the little shotgun house down on Star Street that she and Roy Gene rented from Bill McLaughlin. She was ironing. She looked up to find Jesus standing beside her looking tall and blond like Wayne Morris in the movies. He called her by name and sat down at her kitchen table with her for an hour talking about heaven and sin and the Baptist church that Edna Earle grew up in over in Honey Grove. He took one of her forks and with a tine drew a picture of the throne of God on her oilcloth tablecloth. Then he just disappeared.

Everybody in Bodark who knew Edna Earle came to look at the picture that Jesus drew on her tablecloth. Some said it was an inspired representation from the hand of God, but some said a third grader at the Stonewall Jackson Elementary School could have made a better picture of a throne. Mamie Dell made Tommy Earl go down to Star Street one afternoon after school just to talk to Edna Earle Morris. He came home half scared and half hypnotized. He was scared of being so close to the presence of the Lord, but was struck dumb by Edna Earle's beauty. When Mamie asked him what Edna Earle had told him, he said he didn't exactly remember. He just kept humming, "How Beautiful Heaven Must Be." Mamie thought the boy was overwhelmed by Jesus's effect on Edna Earle and that the humming was in preparation for declaring himself for Christ when Mount Hebron Church had its next revival. Grady figured the boy had been addled by being so close to Edna Earle and that the hymn humming was a sign that puberty might be around the corner.

All the men in town talked about how pretty Edna Earle was. But most of them said something like, "She ain't got much brains, but Lord God is she pretty!"

While Tarp was telling his story, Grady was thinking about how mad he had been when Mamie sent Tommy Earl down there to hear about Jesus.

"Did you hear what I just said?" Tarp asked Grady.

"Yeah, you said Edna Earle Morris was missing."

"Hell, you wasn't listening. You was thinking about how pretty that girl was."

Grady caught Tarp's use of the past tense, "Why did you say 'was?' Do you think she's dead or something?"

Tarp looked pained. "Of course she's dead. You didn't hear a word I said did you? Sheriff Wells has looked all over the county for her body. Now they have brought in that Texas Ranger from over at Bonham, one of the ones that killed Clyde Barrow. They plan to start dragging the creeks around town and then branch out from there."

Grady looked down at the counter while he tried to decide whether to tell Tarp where Edna Earle was. It would all come out sooner or later anyhow, so he figured he might as well tell Tarp now and get it over with.

"Now, Tarp, don't you fall into hollering when I tell you what I'm gonna tell you. Do you hear?"

"Yeah, I hear. What you gonna tell me?"

"Well, Edna Earle ain't dead. She was—"

"Ain't dead! How the hell—"

Grady said, "Will you shut up? You said you wouldn't yell and take on if I told you something. Now are you gonna do what you said you was?"

Tarp leaned close and whispered, "Yeah. Of course I am. Now go on. How do you know she ain't dead?"

"'Cause she's out at my house asleep right now," Grady said.

"Out at your—" Tarp jumped up off the stool, but Grady pushed him down and said, "Will you shut the hell up?"

"Yeah, yeah, okay, but how come? Where's Mamie? Did you and Edna Earle—"

"No, me and Edna Earle didn't do nothing. Nothing like that. Sunday night me and Mamie went up to the Briar Patch. You know, that little joint that Ed Butts just opened up on the Red River?"

"Yeah, yeah," Tarp said, "What about it?"

"Well, on the way home, just when we was coming up the bluff where the road bends to the right, I saw something pink laying in the road. I slammed on the brakes and run off in the ditch to miss it. When I got out and went back up on the road, I seen a woman laying right in the middle of the road wearing nothing but a slip. It was Edna Earle. She said she wanted to get run over and killed. She commenced to crying and hollering and saying how she had been betrayed and how she wanted to die and join her Lord, and how she—"

Tarp couldn't wait to hear more. He broke in with, "Betrayed. By who? Jesus? Is that what she meant? Did she think the Lord should have took her with him when he was—"

Now it was Grady who cut in. "No, it wasn't Jesus. It was that sorry damned Chick Bailey. Her and Chick run off and went to Oklahoma and stayed in a tourist court in Durant until Chick told her he wasn't gonna take her to California with him after all. Then he brought her back across the river on the ferry and put her out. That's when she decided to take off her good dress and lay it beside the road and get herself killed in that pink petticoat. She wanted to save her good white dress that Roy Gene had bought her after Jesus come. She wanted to be buried in it. I guess Chick went on to California like he planned to."

Tarp said, "Well, I'll be a son of a bitch. What you gonna do with her?"

"I don't know. When I get in this evening, I guess I'll take her out to her daddy's place. He lives out close to Savoy. Then it won't be my problem. I hate to have to go up to the sheriff's office and tell what I know, but I guess Herman Wells needs to send that Ranger on back to Bonham or wherever he come from."

Grady got up to go pay Bear for his breakfast, but Tarp called him back and said, "Hey, Grady, who do you think it was that come to Edna Earle's last summer? You know when she was ironing and wearing nothing but that petticoat?"

Grady came back and stared a Tarp a minute. "What? I don't know, but I 'spect it was Jesus, Tarp."

Grady turned and walked away quickly to hide his laughter.

Tarp sat in front of Modell's window with his mouth hanging open. He couldn't believe that Grady Dell had swallowed Edna Earle's loony story about Jesus.

Telling Tarp it was Jesus put a spring in Grady's walk that had been missing for three months. Outside, he began whistling "I Come to the Garden Alone" and suddenly changed to "How Beautiful Heaven Must Be." The rain had stopped, and the sun was trying to break through. Hell, he thought, I may make it through the day. Maybe even the week. Shoot, if it keeps on being this much fun around here, I may live to see 1939.

SEVEN

Confessions

1938

The coldest rain of the year was pouring down on Eastis County as Mamie Dell and Edna Earle Morris sat in Mamie's kitchen smoking Kool cigarettes and drinking Eight O'Clock coffee from the A&P store. At the same exact hour, Grady Dell was in the Busy Bee Cafe telling Tarp Davidson how he and Mamie had found Edna Earle lying in the middle of Highway 5 in a pink petticoat trying to get run over and killed.

Edna Earle coughed and said, "I hate these Kool cigarettes, Mamie. Ain't you got nothing else to smoke?"

"Naw, honey, I don't smoke nothing but Kools. I read where the menthol in Kools clears out your bronchial tubes and soothes the lungs. Just think of how good Mentholatum feels when you rub it on your chest. Didn't you ever try that, honey?"

"No, Momma always made a poultice of mustard and some terrible smelling stuff to smear on us, and then she put a flannel rag on our chests that nearly burned you up."

"Did that help, Edna Earle?"

"I don't think so, but Momma said her momma and grandma always did that and if it was good enough for the Farleys it was good enough for us. But I never could see that it done no good. Don't Grady have nothing to smoke that ain't so freezing to the lungs?"

Edna Earle liked Old Golds because the package looked so ladylike and was so rich in color. And there were the coins on the package. Gold coins. Roy Gene smoked Camels, which is what Edna Earle thought white trash smoked. Chick Bailey smoked Fatimas, which you had to go all the way to Sherman to buy. Chick bought Fatimas by the carton, and Edna Earle had never seen anybody with that many cigarettes at one time. Edna Earle loved Fatimas, but when Chick abandoned her to go off to California or wherever he went, she vowed right then and there never to let a whiff of Fatima smoke pass her lips, nostrils, or lungs. She did that just before taking off her good dress and lying down on the highway to get killed.

Mamie said, "Well, Grady always smokes Camels or Lucky Strikes unless we are out of money. Then he buys Bugler. Come to think of it, there may be a package of Bugler and some papers here somewhere. Let me see."

Mamie left the kitchen and Edna Earle sucked the life out of the last of her Kool before stubbing it out in the ashtray and making a face.

"God Almighty, but that tastes awful," she said out loud. "I'd rather eat shit and run rabbits than smoke them things." She had picked that up from Roy Gene, who was always threatening to eat shit and run rabbits.

"What did you say, honey?" Mamie said from the living room. She was scrabbling through drawers hoping to find Grady's Bugler so she could get back to Edna Earle and get the whole story of her love affair with Chick Bailey. Maybe the right smoke would open Edna Earle up. Smoking always made Mamie feel free, and when John Houston smoked the way he did, Mamie wanted to rip off his clothes wherever they were. John Houston was the most sophisticated man Mamie had ever met.

Nobody in Bodark Springs wore his clothes, carried his cane, or smoked like John Houston. He always took in a mouthful of smoke, let some of it out, and then sucked it up his nostrils. He called it French inhaling, and Mamie always said to herself, "God, that is sexy!"

John and his wife Betty owned the local Ben Franklin store, but Betty did most of the work. John mostly wandered around town dressed in a suit and tie and carrying his cane. In winter, he wore a very long overcoat with raglan sleeves. Judge McCraney said, "John Houston is the only man in Texas who is not crippled or queer who can carry a cane." John's cane was not one of the fancy ebony numbers with a gold head that Fred Astaire danced around in the movies, but rather an old-fashioned, bent-headed walking stick of the kind that the army used to give wounded veterans after the war. John had been in the war, but as far as anybody knew, he hadn't been shot up. He just liked something to lean on when he paused to visit people on the street or to rest his chin on when he sat in a cane chair just inside the Ben Franklin. And John Houston always wore a dark grey fedora with the brim turned up all the way around like Franklin D. Roosevelt wore his. In fact, Mamie thought John looked a lot like a young Franklin D.

Mamie began thinking of John Houston and forgot Edna Earle for a minute. She forgot she had even asked Edna Earle what she had said and only came back to the present when the girl in the kitchen said, "I didn't say nothing. Or maybe I was just talking to myself. I get so lonesome nowadays that I talk to myself a lot. You know I used to talk to Jesus before I took up with that damned Chick Bailey and broke Roy Gene's heart. Probably broke Jesus's, too. He ain't ever been back to see me, you know. But I know Jesus loves me in spite of what I done with Chick."

Mamie had found the Bugler and was rolling Edna Earle a

cigarette, hoping the confessional spell wouldn't be broken. Mamie licked the gummed edge and lit the Bugler cigarette and handed it to Edna Earle.

"Here, try this, honey. I know how it is to break somebody's heart and how it feels to get your own broke, too. How come you and Chick took up in the first place?"

"Mamie, it was love at first sight. I took a look at Chick when he was wearing that bathing suit out at Grant's Mill that time. I just about fainted. Did you ever see Chick in a bathing suit? My God, Mamie, he had the biggest arms and chest you ever saw. And hair all over him. And them swimming trunks, Mamie, they was so tight you could see everything he had. I mean—"

Edna Earle paused and began to cry a little. Not big sobs. Just sniffles, a tear or two, and a quiet sigh.

"What was you saying about the bathing suit, hon?"

"Oh, you know, Mamie, Chick Bailey was very large. I mean in the bathing suit. And, well, you know, out of it, too." Edna Earle mixed a sniffle with a slight giggle. "Roy Gene was a sweet person and bought me lots of things when he could, but Roy Gene didn't have no sex appeal, if you know what I mean."

"You mean he wasn't interested in, in . . . you know."

"Oh, he was. He really was. I mean, well, he was interested in what I could do for him, but he didn't think it was all right for me to like . . . well, you know . . . to like it."

"You mean, for you to like it, too? I sure do know what you mean. Oh, honey, I do. I really do. I mean lots of men just want what is good for them and then they want to turn over and go to sleep. I know what you mean."

"You do?"

Mamie sighed largely and loudly and said, "Oh, Edna Earle, it's a terrible thing to be laying in bed all worked up after a man has gone to sleep. Oh, my God, do I know. What did Chick do that was different?"

"Mamie, he cared about how things were going for me. He asked me all the time when we were together in . . . you know . . . in the bed, how it was for me and whether I was liking it and all. And he waited and waited, and, oh, God, Mamie, I was just in heaven for the three months that Chick kept coming around. Heaven! Pure heaven!"

Edna Earle smoked the Bugler and made a mess of trying to roll another one. Mamie had to take the papers and makings and twirl up another smoke for her.

Lord knows, Edna Earle thought, Lord knows I do need a cigarette. And as much coffee as I can swallow. And then I am going to kill myself again.

"Mamie, have you ever thought about killing yourself?"

"I guess I have a few times, but then something always made me change my mind. You sure don't want to do that again, Edna Earle. Think how your folks would feel with you dead and gone."

"Oh, Mamie, sometimes I think how my funeral would be and how all the people who knew me and grew up out by us would pass by the coffin and see me a-laying in a white dress. I am sure Momma would dress me all in white, like the dress I laid down on the highway."

"Even after you run off with Chick Bailey and all?"

"Well, Mamie, I think when you are dead, everybody will forget about what you done in life, and I think Jesus would be waiting for me on the other side if I was real sorry about what I done."

"I'm sure he would honey, but you don't want to be talking about dying, as young as you are."

"Mamie, haven't you ever thought about what will happen when you die? How all the people will cry and take on? Don't you ever plan for a fine funeral with Mr. Thurman Whitmire putting you in one of his fine caskets and then people coming to look at your body? I know I do."

Mamie said, "Edna Earle, I don't care what they do to me when I am gone. They can just sharpen my feet and drive me in the ground for all I care."

"Well I don't see it that way a-tall. I want a nice funeral with wreaths and all."

Edna Earle considered herself to be a successful suicide even though Grady Dell had picked her up off the two-lane highway that runs between Bodark and Bonham and put her in the back seat of the Chevrolet that he and Mamie were driving back from the Century Club. Edna Earle had been completely drunk, slobbering drunk, when they found her lying in the middle of the highway crying and saying, "Go ahead on. Go ahead on. Run over me and kill me. Just go ahead on."

When Grady picked Edna Earle up and forced her, kicking and crying, into the back seat of the car, he had been a little past his normal "three sheets to the wind," the level he considered most pleasant and most memory-erasing. Mamie, as usual, hadn't had a drop. She never drank. "I don't drink nothing but Co-Cola," Mamie repeated a hundred times a night at the Century Club or the Silver Slipper or the Hop Rite Inn or wherever she and Grady went for an evening of serious honky-tonking. Mamie was proud of her Baptist teetotalling status, though she hadn't been inside a Baptist church since she and Grady married in 1922. Grady was an ordained elder in the Presbyterian Church, but she had been inside the churches of that denomination not more than ten times in the sixteen years they had been married. Grady tried for a time to hew to the Presbyterian line, but after a few years of whiskey and Mamie and honky-tonks and late nights and overwork, he had become as scant in his church presence as Mamie. And while Mamie made it a point to tell every new acquaintance, and most of the old ones, that she never let a drop of whiskey pass her lips, everybody in Bodark Springs knew that Mamie ingested more prescription drugs than anybody in Eastis

County, once John Carmichael had left town. Carmichael was the town's first known dope fiend, but his family had money and paid him to move on to Dallas. Mamie swallowed at least a dozen Stanback Headache Powders a day on top of prescription drugs she got from doctors in Paris, Bonham, Sherman, Dekalb, and Clarksville. These drugs were over and above a large volume from Dr. Clayton and Old Dr. Elgin right here in Bodark Springs. And Grady couldn't count the times he had had to call Dr. Clayton at two o'clock in the morning so he could give Mamie a shot of morphine for one of her jumping headaches or any number of other maladies that came in the night. But Mamie had no sympathy for anybody who resorted to alcohol. She went where they sold both "white whiskey," the homemade kind, and red whiskey that said "bottled in bond." Red whiskey was sneaked into the county by whiskey runners getting rich off the dry laws of Northeast Texas. White whiskey was made by old boys with car radiators and iron kettles and copper tubing out in the woods. Mamie tolerated Grady's drinking, but not with a good grace. Years later, Tommy Earl said, "Momma drove Daddy to drink and gave him hell every day of his life for drinking." He repeated his father's line when he added, "Momma could smell a sip of whiskey over the telephone."

But Mamie was in no mood to chastise Edna Earle for being drunk the night before. After all, maybe Edna Earle's hangover would loosen her tongue, and Mamie could get more juicy details about the talked-about Chick Bailey.

Mamie handed Edna Earle another Bugler cigarette and said, "Honey, I think I know what you was going through with Roy Gene. I have had me a little dose"—she pronounced it "dost"—"of that over the last sixteen years."

"You mean Grady don't do you no more good than Roy Gene done me?"

"That is exactly what I mean, and just like you done, I found me somebody who could give me a little relief once in a while."

Edna Earle liked gossip as well as anybody else—everybody else—in Bodark Springs, Texas. So her ears perked up at what she hoped would be Mamie's tales of hidden love and illicit sexual encounters. She waited for Mamie to go on, and when she didn't, Edna Earle said, "Who?"

"Oh, hon, I can't say another word."

"But I told you all about me and Chick Bailey."

"Yeah, I know, honey, but you have already run off and left Roy Gene and everybody knows about you and Chick. But I am still here at home with Grady and these two young'uns, so my lips are sealed up tight, if you know what I mean."

"Is it John Houston?" Edna Earle was pretty sure it was, for there had been talk at the Pandora Beauty Salon about Mamie and John Houston being seen one night in Sherman when Grady was in Fort Worth for a meeting of the Rural Letter Carriers' Association. But nobody was sure that Betty Houston wasn't with them and was maybe just in the restroom. But tales grew about Mamie and John as tales always grew in Depression-era Bodark Springs when so many people were out of work and time was well spent attacking reputations.

Mamie thought about all that Edna Earle had told her and decided that the two of them had so much in common that she could make a clean—or dirty—breast of things. "Edna Earle, I am going to tell you something, but you have to swear on a stack of Bibles that you won't ever tell a soul. Do you hear me?"

"Oh, Mamie, I am deaf and dumb when it comes to keeping secrets. So you can tell me anything you want to and I won't tell a soul. I will cross my heart."

Edna Earle crossed her heart twice. And behind her back she crossed her fingers.

Mamie said, "Well, I have been in love with John Houston for about three years, and me and him slip off whenever we can and go to that tourist court over in Grayson County. The one they call Rose Hill Tourist Cabins. Do you know the place?"

"Oh, God, do I. That is where me and Chick went two or three times. I love that place. It is so romantic."

"Well, me and John go over there when Miss Betty is busy at the Ben Franklin and Grady is on one of his long days. You know he has short days and long days, don't you?"

"What?"

"Well, on short days he mostly delivers here in Eastis County, but on the long days, he has a route that runs way over into Fannin. On them days, he don't get home much before five o'clock. And so then me and John has what I call a 'looong day.' If you know what I mean. Then, we can stay out till four or so, and I can rush home and put something in the pressure cooker so Grady will think I have been slaving all day. He never knows what hit him. Or maybe I should say what hits me! Now, you promise you won't ever tell a soul. Remember. You crossed your heart."

"Oh, I did. I did! Reckon you could roll me another one of them Bugler cigarettes?"

EIGHT

Four Roses Whiskey

1939

Grady Dell almost always stopped at the last house on his mail route, got out, went in, and visited for ten or fifteen minutes. Today, he hurriedly put two letters and a copy of the *Progressive Farmer* in the mailbox and started to pull away, hoping nobody inside had seen him. Just as he got his 1938 Chevy up out of the ditch and angled into the road, he heard Henry's voice.

"Grady! Ho, Grady. Hold up a minute."

Grady hadn't noticed his older brother, who was coming through the gate across the road from the house. Henry was wearing overalls and a heavy jumper and carrying two rabbits by the ears in his left hand, his rifle in his right.

"Wasn't you gonna stop and see Mammy? You know she could die any day. Hell, Grady, she's eighty—or she will be this summer. And she's done had two strokes, and you know what they say?"

"About what?"

"About strokes. The third one kills you, they say. So you ain't coming in?"

"No, not today. I'm running late. I guess I better get on in to the post office and check up."

"Get in early so you can run by Tubby Wallace's to get you a drink of whiskey? Is that what the hurry is?"

Grady blushed. That was exactly what he planned to do. It was what he did every day. And he had been stopping by Tubby's trailer house to get a water glass half full of Four Roses ever day since August of 1936, the month and the year he got so far into debt that he lost his house and had to move Mamie and the kids upstairs over the pressing shop in Bodark.

But he lied to Henry, "No, I ain't going by Tubby Wallace's. I told you I'm running late. Melvin's after me to get my outgoing mail in before three o'clock. He likes to get it down to the station so he can knock off at five. Did you ever see it this cold in January?"

Grady wanted Henry off the subject of Tubby Wallace, who was sitting in a warm trailer on no-telling-how-many gallons of bootlegged blended whiskey just six miles out of Bodark, on the highway to Bonham. Grady sighed when Henry opened the door on the passenger side of Grady's new 1938 Chevrolet and climbed in, dead rabbits still in his left hand.

"Come on, Henry! Don't be dripping blood all over the seats of my new car. I ain't had it more 'n a month or so and you know it."

"I ain't gonna get no blood on your seats. Them rabbits is nearly froze stiff from being carried a mile in that weather. But if you want to talk about the weather, I've seen it colder in January. Lots of times."

Henry knew Grady wasn't worried about the weather and had just brought it up to change the subject. He looked over at his younger brother and said, "Mammy's worried about you. Says you look worse and worse every time you come in the house. More hangdog, she says. I think it's more hangover, but I don't say nothing about hangovers to Mammy. Lon Marshall said the other day that you looked like you had been shot at and missed and shit at and hit."

"Lon Marshall is a sorry bastard, one of the sorriest bastards in Texas."

Henry nodded his head, "Yeah, he's sorry all right. But he ain't far from wrong about you. You're what? Forty-seven, forty-eight now?"

"Forty-seven. I'm still just ten years younger than you. You ought to be able to keep track of that."

"You look ten years older; did you know that?"

Grady Dell sighed. Henry was right, and Henry had a right to say it. Taking care of their mother gave him the right. Being head of the family in a part of the world where family meant a great deal gave him the right.

"What do you plan to do, drink yourself to death before you're fifty?"

"I take a little drink once in a while, but I just do it to steady my nerves."

"You ought to have 'em pretty steady now from what I hear."

"Goddammit, Henry—" But Grady stopped himself when he remembered how Henry and his wife Flora had put up a bed in the living room of their two-room unpainted shack so that Mammy could have their room. He said in a more moderate voice, "I don't have to drink, you know. I don't just lay drunk all the time. I mean, I just take a drink once in a while to steady—"

"Yeah, I know. Just to steady your nerves. Was your nerves steady last Saturday night when you and J. T. offered to whip the house up at the Silver Slipper?"

"Who told you that?" Grady was startled to find out that Henry was getting the honky-tonk gossip. He thought Henry and Flora lived too far out in the country to hear such talk.

"It don't matter who told me. What matters is that you and J. T. could have both got yourself killed offering to whip them tie hackers and timber haulers. What was it about?"

"It wasn't nothing. Look, Henry, tell Mammy I'll stop by tomorrow. I got to get on now. Melvin likes to get the mail over to—"

"Yeah, I know, Grady. He likes to get it over to the T&P. I'm sorry I was so hard on you. You come on by tomorrow."

Henry opened the door and got out. Then he leaned back in and said, "Damn, Grady, since Grover died last year, you the only brother I got. And Mammy won't be with us long. I can tell. I just don't want you to get into more trouble—well, you know."

Grady had his head bowed over the steering wheel, looking down at the odometer of his car and reading the 21,000 miles that it showed while Henry climbed out of the car. He looked up at Henry and said, "Yeah, Henry, I know. I won't do anything dumb. It's just that—I don't know—everything seems to happen at once, and if it ain't one thing, it's another. You know?"

Henry closed the door and leaned in, "Yeah, I know, Grady, just be careful. That's all I ask."

Grady said, "I will." Then he rolled up the window, started the car, and pulled out into the road.

When Grady Dell reached Highway 5, he turned east and, as he liked to think to himself, "headed for the barn." The barn was the new WPA-built post office in Bodark Springs, Texas, the county seat of Eastis County. Eastis is one of the half-dozen counties south of the Oklahoma line—the Red River—in Northeast Texas. State Highway 5 and the T&P Railroad run side by side about fifteen miles south of the Red and pass through the middle of every county in the northeastern tier—Bowie, Red River, Lamar, Fannin, Eastis, and Grayson. Both roads come into the state at Texarkana and describe a flattened arc as they pass through the county seats: Clarksville, Paris, Bonham. Bodark Springs, and Sherman. Highway 5 keeps going to Wichita Falls where it angles off to the southwest and heads across West Texas to Lubbock. And then it swings sharply southwest and then west toward Lovington, New Mexico. The T&P is not so ambitious. It goes only as far west as Whitesboro in Grayson County before turning south for Fort Worth.

Grady Dell knew every back road north of 5 in Eastis and Fannin Counties and most of the unpaved pig trails in the top halves of both Lamar and Red River. He had ridden them horseback when he was a teenager hunting and fishing along the Red. Then, as a young man, he had courted in a buggy all over the top half of Northeast Texas. Now, as a mail carrier, he put in 30,000 miles a year hauling the mail over the back roads of half of Eastis County and half of Fannin. And he estimated that he still put in 8,000 night miles a year hitting all the honky-tonks on both sides of the Red. Grady did all his driving north of the T&P and State Highway 5. For some reason that he didn't understand, he had an aversion to everything south of those two arteries—or veins, depending on how you looked at it. The merchants along the twin roads saw them as highways bringing in goods to be sold. But Grady thought of the roads as escape routes for the young. For nearly twenty years—ever since he had come back from the war in 1919—every kid that he had watched grow up couldn't wait to set out for Dallas to make a fortune or get into trouble. Or both. Nobody seemed willing to stay in country villages like English or Rowena or Novice, and most weren't even satisfied with small cities like Honey Grove, Bonham, and Bodark Springs. Somehow Grady couldn't really imagine living anywhere but in Eastis County—or Fannin maybe. And Grady had seen New York, London, Paris, and Brussels. The song that said, "How're you gonna keep 'em down on the farm after they've seen Paree?" made no sense to Grady Dell.

He no longer hunted and fished the river bottoms of the Red and the Sulphur, but he had them at hand if he wanted to.

For Grady, everything north of the T&P was new and fresh and washed clean, even when it wouldn't rain for two months and the roads got so dusty that a small wind would blind you with red dirt as you drove along. Even when the Red River was dry enough to plow, Grady had a feeling that it was washing the country clean. He could sit in his car in the heat of August and look down the bank above the dwindling stream—hardly big enough to call a river by some standards—and think that the "old" Red was washing Fannin and Eastis and Red River Counties clean. And in some ways Grady thought the dirty river was washing him clean, too, taking his weakness for beer and whiskey and women down the stream to wherever it was that the Red went. Was it the Mississippi? Or was it the Gulf of Mexico? He always meant to ask his daughter Jackie to look it up for him in school, but he seemed always to forget.

Grady had a funny feeling about those parts of the Red River counties that were south of the T&P and State 5. The people seemed different, the land softer and more worn. The black waxy prairies ran south of the twin roads, and the people down there had more money and an easier living. North of 5 was hardscrabble country, and the people who lived up there were tough Scotch-Irish who were closer to the rootstock of the South than the inhabitants of the south part of the counties. If you made a dollar in the hardscrabble country, it came the hard way—from hacking ties or row cropping or making a little white whiskey. You grew your food or you shot it or you fished for it. You didn't buy much of it at the grocery store. These were the people that Grady had grown up with, and he understood them better than he did the town folks and the more prosperous farmers in the south halves of "his" counties. Or so Grady thought.

Grady dreaded the thought that he would soon have to drive up to the post office lugging his sacks and the undelivered COD parcels in under the disapproving eye of Melvin Spruille. Melvin had been made postmaster when Franklin D. Roosevelt took office in 1933. Grady had liked it better when Jack Hurst had been postmaster all during the Republican years of the twenties. Melvin had been postmaster when Grady got his civil service job during the Woodrow Wilson administration. But when Harding beat Cox, Melvin was out, and Jack Hurst, the only Republican in Bodark Springs, was in. Postmasters were not civil service jobs and changed with the political winds.

Jack Hurst was a friendly man who could take a joke, but Melvin was dry and sour. Everybody who knew him well always said, "That Melvin Spruille is a son of a bitch." He gloried in Prohibition and was sorry to see the Eighteenth Amendment repealed when FDR got in office. He was doing all he could to keep Texas dry. He couldn't manage all 254 counties, but he was doing all he could to keep Eastis County dry as a bone.

Grady knew Melvin had noticed his hangover this morning when he got to the post office to sort his mail. And he knew Melvin would be watching him this afternoon to see if he had stopped by Tubby's trailer. Grady thought, if the damned Baptists and bootleggers didn't run this county, a man could get a drink and not have to pay three prices for a shot of Four Roses. Melvin and his church house friends were making Tubby Wallace rich. No telling how much money Tubby paid the "drys" to make it so a man couldn't even get a legal bottle of beer in this county. Then he laughed to himself. He got all the beer he wanted. There must have been twenty honky-tonks along the Red River that sold that Oklahoma 3.2 beer. You could sit at a table as pretty as you please and drink even though it was against the law. Hell, these honky-tonks and assorted bootleggers were making Sheriff Herman Wells rich. There was an old Texas saying, "All you need to be a millionaire in Texas is to serve one term as sheriff of a dry county."

Grady drove west on Highway 5 at a steady forty miles an hour, looking off to the south at the stubble of cotton fields frozen solid in this hard freeze. The sheets of ice in the fields looked like mirrors under a dead-gray sky. Grady tried to take an interest in the landscape, but his mind kept turning to how warm it would be in Tubby's trailer house and how warm the Four Roses would be in his stomach when Tubby poured his "big shot" in the back room he had partitioned off for sit-down drinkers. Not that Grady was a sit-down drinker. He usually stepped behind the partition and stood there as Tubby poured the glass a little more than half full for Grady. Then Grady would take his left hand and hold his nose with it as he took the glass in his right hand and drained it down in one long gasping swallow. Then with a shudder and a strangle, Grady would set the glass down and pay Tubby the dollar he charged for a double shot.

Tubby was always generous to Grady, for they were veterans of the same war. Grady had gone over as an infantryman in the First Division and Tubby had been a machine gunner in the 42nd Rainbow Division. Their outfits fought side by side across France, and both Tubby and Grady had been gassed when the Germans got desperate in 1918. Tubby was a hero who had got "shot all to pieces" in the Argonne Forest near Nantillois. That was one reason Herman Wells left him alone to sell bootleg whiskey. That was just one reason. The other was that Tubby paid Wells ten percent of what he made so that he could stay in business.

Grady had been a hero, too, but he always kept quiet about his part in whipping the Kaiser. Grady and Clint Carter, an old coon hunter from Fannin County, had wiped out a German machine gun nest in the Argonne Forest near Cunel. Their corporal said it made it possible for the remnants of the 18th infantry regiment to get out of the woods alive. That is how his war had been. But Grady had no medals except the French Croix de Guerre that the whole division got. Nor did he want any. Mostly, Grady wanted to forget those ten German children that he and Clint killed. They shot seven and Grady bayoneted two before he saw that they were not grown men. They were fifteen-year-old boys who got called up when the war was going badly for Germany. Clint had just stabbed the tenth German when Grady saw what they had done and screamed, "God in heaven, Clint, look who we have killed!"

Grady never got over it.

Those were thoughts that ran through Grady's head as he got close to the cutoff that led to Tubby's trailer. As he turned up the road that led to Tubby's, he always stopped thinking about the war and began to worry that somebody might see him as he went in to get a drink. There must not have been three grownups in Eastis County who didn't know that Grady was drinking all the time now, but he fooled himself that he only drank a little and hardly anybody knew. It was against the rules for a government employee to drink on the job, and Grady could almost argue himself into the idea that since he had delivered the last piece of mail, he was legally or technically—or theoretically if you thought about it—off the job. At least in the sight of God. But he wasn't. And he knew it.

Grady hoped every time he pulled into Tubby's clearing that all he would see was Tubby's 1938 LaSalle coupe sitting under the big hackberry. Tubby had the finest car in Eastis County. It was a LaSalle "doctor's car," and though Doc Clayton had one it was a year older than Tubby's. Clayton had as much money as Tubby, but he didn't want to drive a better car than his own bootlegger. Tubby always said, "Well, I guess I practice as much medicine as old Clayton, so it's only right for me to drive a 'doctor's car.'"

Today, Tubby's car sat alone. Grady breathed a sigh of relief as he pulled in beside the big V8. He got out of his car for the first time since he had left the post office in the morning, groaned, stretched, and hobbled up to Tubby's door. Tubby had seen him coming, so as soon as Grady raised his hand to knock, Tubby hollered out, "Come on in, Grady. You gonna freeze out there in this weather."

Grady stepped inside the door and limped toward the coal stove that Tubby had sitting in the middle of the room. "How come you limpin', Grady? You didn't fall down last Saturday night up at the Silver Slipper, did you?"

"Damn, Tubby, does everybody in the county know every move I make?"

"Might near. After all, everybody knows you, being as you're the mail carrier and all. What's really the matter with your leg?"

"It's just gone to sleep. Does it everyday. I guess I sit in one spot too long. I probably ought to get out and walk around once in a while, but I don't usually stop till I get to Henry's."

"You seen Dr. Clayton about it?"

"Naw, Tubby, it usually goes away when I walk around a little."

Tubby rocked back on the legs of the straight chair he sat in. "Your momma had a stroke of paralysis didn't she?"

"Yeah, she's had two," Grady mumbled. Then in a clear voice he said, "You saving that whiskey you got in the back room for something, or do you think you might sell somebody a drink of it?"

Tubby heaved his three hundred pounds out of the chair and headed for the back room. He scrabbled around in a footlocker and came out with a quart of Four Roses, the only bonded whiskey anybody ever drank in Eastis County. Then he reached up on a shelf and brought down a barrel-shaped water glass that must have weighed half a pound and poured it three-fourths full for Grady. Grady reached for it and for his nose at the same moment. Then he drank it off in one choking swallow.

After shuddering a little, he put the glass back down on the table. Tubby said, "I-God, I wouldn't take on like that if I was to drank carbolic of acid."

"Me neither if it was carbolic of acid. But bad or good, it will do to get me through the rest of this freezing day."

"Grady, about that leg of yours—"

"Now, Tubby, there ain't nothing wrong with that leg. It just goes to sleep if I sit in the car too long."

"Does it stay numb after it wakes?"

"Aw, it tingles a little bit most of the time, but it ain't nothing to worry about. If I didn't sit all day long in that damned Chevy, it wouldn't always go to sleep. Besides, cold as it is now, everybody tingles some."

"Now, Grady, I ain't no doctor, but I ain't no damn fool neither. If it was me, I would go see old Clayton about it. You might be fixin' to have a stroke of paralysis like your momma done."

"Naw. I'm all right. How much do I owe you?"

"A dollar, like always."

"You poured it pretty full today. I thought you might be running me a dollar-and-a-quarter drink today."

"You look like you needed a little something extra. Besides, us old vets have to look after one another sometimes."

Grady put his hat on and buttoned up his overcoat and said, "I'll see you in a few days, Tubby."

"Hell, you'll see me tomorrow," Tubby said to himself after Grady had shut the door.

Grady felt like a new man after all four of the roses had put a little color in his cheeks and kicked his circulation to life. His leg had lost most of its tingle and he thought he might be able to face Mamie and the kids if he could get by Melvin and Charlie Stone, the window clerk, those two hard-core hypocrites and prohibitionists.

Well, it won't be long now, Grady thought. Tubby's was just four miles out from Bodark Springs. It was easy driving distance for the thirsty, but far enough out so that the church ladies wouldn't see every car that drove up to Tubby's. Grady made it to the city limits in eight minutes and was turning into the square a minute later. He took out the package of Sen-Sen that he always carried and popped two in his mouth. Then he eased his car into his slot at the side of the post office. He sat there with the motor running as he thought about his mother and Henry and his brother Grover Cleveland who died last year. He thought about his father and his uncle Hut and the mules that ran away and killed his father in 1923. He thought about the German boys he and Clint had killed twenty years before. His leg didn't hurt anymore, but somehow he couldn't reach up and turn off the switch key. He thought, I'll turn it off in a minute. I'd turn it off right now if I had a little something to steady my nerves.

While he was sitting thinking about the switch key and the motor running, Henry's old 1927 Chevrolet with the Isinglass curtains pulled into the space next to him on his passenger's side. Henry tapped on the glass and said, "Roll the window down, Grady."

Grady wanted to roll the window down, but somehow he couldn't manage it. When he didn't, Henry opened the door and got in.

Grady said in the voice that only he could hear, "I hope he don't have the damn bleeding rabbits."

"Grady, are you all right?" Henry leaned close to him, but Grady didn't—or wouldn't or couldn't—move.

"Grady, it's about Mammy. Are you too goddamn drunk to move your head? I said Mammy had that third stroke about ten minutes after you left to go to Tubby Wallace's to tank up on cheap whiskey. I know you went there because I stopped off in that goddamn trailer and asked Tubby Wallace if you had been there. He didn't want to tell me, but when I told him Mammy was dead, he said, 'Yeah, Henry, he was by and maybe you ought to make him go see old Clayton. He didn't look too good to me.'"

Grady sat staring ahead thinking how warm it was in Tubby's and how much he needed one of Tubby's shots—just one of the "little shots"—about one good swallow. Maybe just a third of a glass of Four Roses.

When Henry reached out to shake Grady, his younger brother just slumped against the driver's side door and sat silent. Henry couldn't hear Grady say, "Just give me a minute. I'll be all right. All I need is a minute to rest. If I had just a little drink to steady my nerves, I could go and see about Mammy."

NINE

It's the Law

1 9 3 9

I

It was a gray, bitter, late-December day in Bodark Springs. It was so cold that Judge McCraney sat behind his desk in the little municipal courtroom with his hat and overcoat on. The judge wasn't holding court; the only other person in the tiny three-room municipal building was Banty Isbell, who, with his twin brother Bunk, shared the roles of city secretary/volunteer fire chief/municipal jailer. One or the other of them usually sat in the outer office waiting for a fire call. Or for somebody to come in to pay a fine for drunkenness. Or for running a stoplight. The third room in the building was an add-on; it had been built by the WPA a year earlier to make a holding cell for miscreants too tame to need sending across the square to Sheriff Herman Wells's jail in the basement of the county courthouse.

Banty was leaning against the doorjamb that led into McCraney's tiny courtroom talking about Hitler. It was a week before Christmas, 1939, and Europe had been at war since September. Banty was saying, "I-God, when England and Britain both gets to fighting, that damned war won't last three months."

Judge James W. McCraney was just pointing out that England and Britain were the same when the door flew open and

Isham B. Hayes, the garageman and mechanic from down the street, came in shivering against the cold.

Hayes didn't waste time on preliminaries: "Judge, what's the fine for assault and battery?"

It seemed an odd question, but Judge McCraney made it a habit never to appear surprised, so he looked at Hayes under lidded, bored eyes and said, "Twenty-five dollars." He wanted to say "Why?" But McCraney chose never to stoop to curiosity.

Hayes, who ran the only decent garage in Bodark Springs—some said in Northeast Texas—ran his hand into the pocket of his coveralls, pulled out a roll of bills, and started counting out ones. When he got to twenty-five, he handed the stack of greasy bills to McCraney and said, "Here's the fine."

"Thank you. I'll get you a receipt." He turned to Banty and said, "Mr. City Secretary, get me a receipt made out to Isham B. Hayes for twenty-five dollars in payment of a fine for assault and battery."

Banty, who was still trying to puzzle out how England and Britain could possibly be the same country, started rustling through the papers in the old desk looking for the receipt book and a pencil. He got the book and an already abused sheet of carbon paper. Then he wetted the lead of his pencil with his tongue so that he could begin slowly and laboriously to fill out the form.

He worked for a while and said, "All right, Judge, I got the receipt made out to I. B. Hayes"—he couldn't spell Isham—"now, what do I put in where it says what the fine's for?"

"Assault and battery."

"Yessir, I know, but who did he assault, Judge?"

Judge McCraney was busy dusting off imaginary specks on his blue serge Hart Schaffner & Marx suit. The judge was a dapper man—some said a dude—with an Errol Flynn mustache. J. W. McCraney was without doubt the best-dressed man in Eastis

County. The only thing that marred his looks was the fact that he was one legged and had to get around on crutches. His left leg was cut off so close to the hip that it was impossible to fit him with a cork leg, but he was so expert with the crutches that he seemed to make them a natural part of him. How he had lost the leg nobody in Bodark knew, though McCraney didn't do anything to quell the rumors that the absent limb had died a hero's death in the First World War and was buried somewhere in the Meuse-Argonne Forest. He had come to Bodark about 1923, so nobody knew for sure how he had got his leg cut off. Everybody was too polite to ask, and McCraney kept his past life to himself. He practiced law for awhile, but gave it up when he ran for—and won—the municipal court judgeship. About 1930, he opened a Texaco station on the best corner in town, but he left the running of it to Eugene Schmitt and spent most of his time sitting in the little two-room city office building or hanging out at Ralph Powers's cafe.

When McCraney didn't answer Banty's question about the reason for the fine, Banty came over to the judge's desk and asked again, "Who did he assault, Judge?" Then he pointed to the pad of receipts and said, "There is a place right here to list the name of the person or persons who are victims of the crime. See, here it is right here," and he turned the paper toward Judge McCraney.

McCraney didn't look at the paper in Banty's hand. He said, "You'll have to ask Hayes here. He didn't tell me."

Banty looked at Isham B. Hayes in his filthy coveralls and then at McCraney, who now sat behind the desk with his only leg propped up on one corner. He looked at Hayes, who stood mute, and at McCraney who was looking off into the middle distance trying hard to affect complete boredom and said, "You been in a fistfight, Isham B.?"

"No."

"Then how come you are charged with assault and battery?"

"I ain't."

"Then how come the Judge here told me to make out a receipt for twenty-five dollars?"

"I don't care nothing about no receipt. I just come up here to pay my fine."

McCraney stood up on his one leg and grabbed his crutches all in the same motion and said to nobody in particular, "I'm going on down to the filling station. If anybody wants me I'll either be there or over at Ralph Powers's."

"Just a minute, Judge," Banty said. "How am I supposed to make out this receipt? How am I supposed to enter this in the fine book?"

"How the hell do I know? I told you—ask Isham B. here."

McCraney paused, but if Hayes didn't volunteer any information, McCraney would have to swing himself out the door without knowing why Hayes was offering to pay a fine for an unsolved and possibly uncommitted misdemeanor. He had gone too far with his boredom to turn back now.

"Melvin Spruille," Hayes said.

"Melv—what the hell are you talking about? Melvin Spru—The postmaster? You hit the goddam post—What the hell do—" the Judge sputtered to a halt and stared goggle-eyed. First at Isham B. Hayes and then at Banty Isbell.

It was too late for McCraney to pretend nonchalance. He had revealed himself and was disgusted at his own outburst. So he turned to Isham B. Hayes and said, his voice now under control, "So you have had a fight with Melvin Spruille. When did this happen? And where?"

"It ain't yet," Hayes said.

"You mean—" Banty and the judge spoke at once, and when Banty stopped in mid sentence, McCraney went on, "You mean to tell me, Isham B., that you are paying a fine for an assault and battery that you plan to commit? That you haven't done anything yet?"

"That's right."

"Well, goddammit, Hayes, you can't just waltz in here to this office and pay a fine and then go off and commit a crime and—" McCraney couldn't find a way to end the sentence.

"Melvin Spruille is a son of a bitch and I am going over to the post office and whip his ass right now. Then Banty here can fill in his blank and let me alone."

Judge James B. McCraney half walked, half hopped back to his desk and fell into the chair again. He looked up at Isham B., who still stood with his legs apart in a truculent stance, and said to him, "Well, goddammit, Hayes, I know Melvin is a son of a bitch. Everybody in Bodark knows that. Nearly everybody in Eastis County must know what kind of son of a bitch Melvin is, but if everybody decided to whip his ass, where would we be then? That's what I want to know."

Both Hayes and Judge McCraney were careful in their pronunciation of "son of a bitch." Neither one used the more casual "sunavabitch" or "sumbitch," so it was clear that they were serious.

They were taken by surprise when Banty answered McCraney's rhetorical question about "where we would be then" by saying, "A whole lot better off, I'd say!" Banty surprised himself by speaking, but caught himself in a second and said, "Excuse me, Judge, but that just slipped out. But, hell, Judge, you know your ownself what kind of sumbitch Melvin is and how bad he needs his ass whipped."

"Oh, hell, I guess so. Go ahead and record the fine, Banty, but Isham B., you had better not go over to the post office to whip Melvin's ass. I think that makes it a federal crime and you'd find your sorry ass over at the federal courthouse in Sherman staring up at Judge Walter D. McIlroy. And old Walter D. ain't an easy judge."

Hayes walked out to the front door of the jail/city office and spat out some Brown's Mule tobacco juice he had been holding since he came into the office. Then he came back in and said to McCraney, "Old Walter McIlroy was raised on a farm not six miles from Melvin's daddy. Hell, he'd probably pay me to stomp Melvin's ass good."

"Probably would at that," McCraney said. Then he turned to Banty and said, "Give Isham B. here his money back. I'm gonna pay that fine for him."

"Say, Judge," Banty said, "I can spare two dollars; how about me getting in on this ass-whipping fine?"

"Okay by me if it's all right with Isham B."

"Well, it ain't all right with me. I saved up that money to pay, and I want the satisfaction of paying and whipping." With that, Isham B. Hayes walked out of the office and made for his garage two blocks down the street.

McCraney grabbed his crutches and started for the door but stopped. "I'd never catch old Hayes, and besides he probably is too smart to whip Melvin on government property. But you keep an eye on Isham and if he starts in on Melvin, run and get me. I'd pay good money to see Isham Hayes whip Melvin's ass."

II

Before dark, every white male in Bodark Springs knew that Isham B. Hayes was going to whip Melvin Spruille's ass. By the next morning, the rest of Bodark's populace—women and children, black and white—had heard the news. By New Year's Eve, every sharecropper and tie hacker and round dancer in Eastis County knew what was in store for Melvin Spruille. On paper,

Melvin was perfect. He was a Baptist and a Democrat and a Mason. He was a personal friend of Sam Rayburn and had met Franklin D. in person when Roosevelt had saluted "the Empire of Texas" at the Centennial Exhibition in 1936. Melvin had been a second lieutenant during the first war but had got no farther than Fort Dix, New Jersey. He was a married man and a stern father to two boys. He paid his taxes and voted Democrat in every election—even when the Catholic Al Smith had run against Hoover in 1928. So, as far as the record went, Melvin Spruille was a perfect citizen of Bodark Springs, Texas, in the year of our Lord 1939.

But there was no doubt in anybody's mind—black, white, poor, rich, honest, crooked—that Melvin Spruille was a son of a bitch. He had proved it a thousand ways. If your post office box rent was a day late, Melvin sealed your box and sent your relief check back to the government. If clerk Charlie Stone came up a penny short at the end of the day, he stayed in the post office till he found his error—once till ten fifteen on a Saturday night. If your letter weighed over an ounce, Melvin would cancel the stamp and then send it back for postage due. He was always the same. A son of a bitch.

Melvin and his brother Lindley ran the Bodark Springs Drugstore, though Melvin only worked in the store a few nights a week to let Lindley off. Melvin had been postmaster for two years during Woodrow Wilson's second term, but when Harding took office in 1921, Melvin was replaced by Jack Hurst and went back to the drugstore that he and Lindley had inherited when Hermann Spruille died from the Spanish flu in 1918. When Roosevelt was inaugurated in 1933, Jack Hurst went back to running his grocery store full-time and Sam Rayburn got Melvin reappointed postmaster.

C. C. Reed, who ran the grocery story next to Bodark Springs Drugstore, once told Grady Dell, the mail carrier, "That son of a bitch you work for is the most stuck up, tight-assed-walking bastard I ever met."

Grady said, "I'm civil service, so I don't exactly work for him."

"But you will admit that he is a mean-spirited son of a bitch, won't you?" C. C. persisted.

"I may be civil service, but I do owe a little bill at the drugstore, so I'm holdin' my fire on that one, C. C."

"Hell, Grady, you owe a big bill here at the grocery store and no telling how much you owe Tubby Wallace the bootlegger."

"Naw, C. C., Tubby don't allow no credit. I'll try to pay you a little something on the first."

When Grady left C. C.'s store, he saw Melvin going into Spruille Drugs and what looked like half the population of Bodark craning their necks to see if today would be the day that Isham Hayes made good on this threat.

Two weeks had passed since Hayes had paid his fine, and nothing had happened. For most of that time, Melvin wasn't in on the secret and wondered why there was always a crowd following him around town. Every morning when Melvin parked his car in front of the post office and went in, thirty or forty people were milling around on the street near the post office. When he left for lunch to drive home, several cars set out after him and drove slowly past his house when he went in to eat.

Melvin's brother Lindley overheard Sam Attaway telling his cousin from over at Savoy about Hayes's threat. Lindley, who liked Melvin about as much as everybody in Bodark Springs did, kept it to himself for a day or two before deciding that he guessed blood was thicker than water—even Melvin's blood. One night when Melvin went into the drugstore to relieve Lindley for supper, Lindley broke down and told his brother what he had heard.

"Melvin, I don't 'spect you know about Isham Hayes and his fine, do you?"

"What fine?"

"Well, Melvin, I hate to bring this up, but I heard that Hayes went in and paid Judge McCraney a twenty-five-dollar fine as advance payment for an assault-and-battery charge."

"Advance payment? Advance payment? Whoever heard of paying a fine in advance? And why do you hate to bring it up, Lindley? You are not making much sense."

"Well, the reason I hate to bring it up, Melvin, is because I heard that Hayes said you were the one he—that he was going to whip your—well, you know."

"No, Lindley, I don't know. I think you are going to have to make yourself clearer. What exactly do I have to do with this greasy man's supposed fine?"

"It's over you, Melvin."

"Lindley, unless you have been stealing drugs and taking them, you had better quit beating around the bush and tell me whatever you are trying to say."

"All right, Melvin, Isham Hayes said that he was going to whip your ass. There!"

"Lindley, I can't—and won't—abide that kind of talk. I have made it clear that—*My* ass! What do you mean *my* ass?"

"Your ass, Melvin. That is what Sam Attaway from over at Savoy told me that Banty Isbell told him. And he said Banty was over at J. W. McCraney's office when Isham Hayes paid the fine and said—and I quote—'I'm gonna whip Melvin Spruille's ass.'"

Lindley Spruille was scared of his older brother, but he was loving every minute of this. "And another thing that Sam Attaway said was—"

"Never mind, Lindley," Melvin said and took his hat and walked out the front door of the store, leaving Lindley with no supper except for the milkshake that he had Bert Curley the soda jerk make for him.

Melvin talked to Orr Starnes, the chief of police, but Starnes, who hated Melvin, said, "Mr. Spruille, there ain't a thing I can do until Hayes makes his move on you. Then, since he has paid his fine already, I can't see much point in arresting him, can you?"

Melvin did, but he couldn't budge Orr Starnes, so he went to see Herman Wells, the county sheriff, who said, "Melvin, unless he whips your ass out in the county somewhere, I can't touch him. I'd say you ought to stay close to home. You ever had any boxing lessons, Melvin?"

Melvin slammed the door on the way out.

III

Things were quiet around the Bodark Springs Post Office throughout the months of January and February. Melvin spent a lot of time watching his clerk, Charlie Stone, and Grady Dell, the rural letter carrier, and Tarp Davidson, the walking city mailman, to see if they were taking any pleasure in the rumors that still ran back and forth across the county. Even Brace Jackman, the postal inspector out of Fort Worth, had heard the tale of Hayes's fine, and when he made one of his surprise inspections early in March, he looked at Melvin, grinned, and said, "Don't look like you been in any fights lately, Spruille. You been behaving yourself?"

Melvin turned away and then back to Jackman and said, "Here are the COD books you asked for."

Grady had a coughing fit, but since he had been gassed in the war, Melvin couldn't prove that he was coughing to suppress his laughter. Charlie Stone dropped his pencil and had to get down under the counter to find it. Tarp Davidson was just getting back from his afternoon rounds and hadn't realized the postal inspector was calling on Bodark Springs.

Tarp looked around and said, "Hey, Brace, looks like you got everybody looking guilty here. Some kind of crime wave going on?"

Jackman grinned at Tarp and said, "Well, it don't look like it's federal; must be some local brouhaha. That right, Melvin?"

Melvin's face had gone from red to white to purple, but all he said was, "Do you need to see the money order receipts, Mr. Jackman?"

After Jackman left, Tarp and Grady and Charlie got more work done than they had since the Germans rolled into Poland.

After that, almost everybody but Melvin and Hayes had lost interest in the threatened ass-whipping until a rainy day in the middle of March. Melvin had been very careful. Every day he dashed from the post office to his car and from his car to the drugstore. He even drove into his garage and pulled the door down before going out the side door of the garage toward his house. But the rain had been going on for three days, and Melvin got careless. Just as he finished locking up the post office on March 15, he took off his glasses, pulled his hat down, and raised his umbrella to shield himself from the blowing rain as he made for his car.

Isham B. Hayes stepped out from behind Melvin's car and hit him with what Grady Dell called a straight right hand, right between the eyes. Melvin's hat flew off, he dropped the umbrella, and Hayes hit him with a left hook to the nose that caused an explosion of blood to hit Hayes and get all over Melvin's windshield. He hit Melvin with another left and used his right hand to keep Melvin from falling. He held Melvin up against Melvin's own car and kept pounding him with his left hand. Hayes later told Grady Dell that he had nearly busted his right hand when he hit Melvin so high up on the forehead with his first punch.

Grady Dell was giving Tarp Davidson a ride home and had already started his car when the fight—or rather the beating, since Melvin had never raised his hands—broke out. Tarp said to Grady, "You reckon we ought to get out and stop I. B. before he beats Melvin to death?"

"Yeah, I guess so, but hold on a minute. I've got to turn the car off and find my umbrella in all that mess on the back seat. I can't afford to catch a fresh cold. I just got over the last one. I don't guess there is a big hurry, is there?"

Tarp grinned and said, "No, not too much, but I guess sooner or later we are going to have to get out in this rain and stop old I. B. unless he wears his arms out from hitting Melvin."

"You are right, Tarp, but all that mechanic work has built up Hayes's arms. Hell, he's got the biggest arms in Bodark, so I guess we got a minute or two before he wears out."

Tarp and Grady got out of Grady's Chevy and walked over to Hayes, who had his victim laid out across the hood of Melvin's 1936 Buick and was now reduced to slapping the inert postmaster.

"That'll do, Isham," Grady said, and pushed Isham away from Melvin.

Hayes was completely docile now. He looked at Tarp and Grady and the crowd that had gathered, huddled back against the post office wall until Grady stopped the fight. Now they all crowded around the hood of Melvin's Buick to see the damage. Hayes looked around and said, "Well, I guess that's about twenty-five dollars' worth, ain't it?" and walked off in the direction of his garage.

Charlie Stone slipped out of the crowd and helped get Melvin across the street to Dr. Clayton's clinic.

Grady and Tarp stood hatless and umbrella-less in the rain, talking to one of the most festive groups Bodark Springs had seen since the war started. Everybody asked the same question: "What was Hayes after Melvin about and why did he wait so long?"

Grady said, "Maybe he was waitin' for the Ides of March," but that didn't get a reaction, and finally everybody drifted off with a story to tell at supper.

It was a month or two before old man C. B. Isbell, Bunk and Banty's father, got Isham B. Hayes to tell him the story.

Hayes said, "It is in nineteen and fourteen and Melvin didn't have so much money then. Remember? He drove that old T-Model Ford with the Isinglass curtains? Well, Mr. Isbell, he sent his brother Lindley after me one night about ten thirty to come and fix that car, said he thought it had a busted magneto. So I drove out to where Melvin was broke down and saw right off what the trouble was. The son of a bitch had run out of gas and was too stupid to know it. So I drove back in and pumped up five gallons and put it in my can and takened it out to Melvin and poured it in his car for him and even cranked the T-Model so he could take that Brasher girl he was sparking on home. Next day, when I went to settle up, I told Melvin that he owed me seventy-five cents for the gas and two dollars for mechanic work. Wellsir, that son of a bitch give me six bits for the gas, but wouldn't pay me a dime for my work. Said his car wasn't broke and didn't need a mechanic. What it needed was a gas man and I had been paid for that. Well, I decided right then and there that I was going to whip Melvin Spruille's ass. And I done it."

Old man Isbell had laughed so much that tears ran down his face, but he finally recovered enough to say, "But you waited twenty-five years or so, Hayes. How come?"

"I waited exactly twenty-five years. To the day. That son of a bitch cheated me on March the fifteenth of nineteen and fourteen, and it was raining, by God. So I waited until I had twenty-five dollars saved up—one for each year—and I waited for it to rain so that son of a bitch would have to take his glasses off. You know, Texas don't let you hit a feller with glasses. It's against the law."

Melvin tried to find a lawyer in Bodark to sue Hayes, but nobody would take the case. Herman Wells said he heard that Melvin had gone to Bonham and Paris and Clarksville trying to get somebody to sue Isham B. Hayes, but, Wells said, "They all knowed what a son of a bitch Melvin was and figured he wouldn't pay up even if he won. Cheap son of a bitch!"

TEN

A Glory Hallelujah Jubilee

1940

In that summer before Pearl Harbor, Tommy Earl Dell was nine years old. And still he had not been saved. Peavine Deerfield, who was in Tommy's room at the Stonewall Jackson Elementary School in Bodark Springs, Texas, had been saved ten or twelve times before he was ten. Tommy Earl had seen Peavine answer the call several times at revivals, and that got him to worrying about when he would get up his nerve to walk down the aisle when some preacher or other issued the call as they sang "Almost Persuaded." Tommy Earl wasn't exactly sure what Peavine meant when he announced several times that he was taking Jesus as his personal savior. "Personal" seemed strange to Tommy Earl, but he reckoned it must be the sure-fire way to get sanctified and be ready for heaven when you died. Peavine not only walked down the aisle at every opportunity, but he had managed to get himself baptized by several Baptist congregations, a Pentecostal church, and even once got sprinkled by some evangelical Methodists. He would have tried out Mormons, Episcopalians, Catholics, and Unitarians except there were none of them in Bodark. The only Catholic in town was Joe Becker, the beauty operator, who had to ride the T&P on Saturday night to make it to mass in Sherman on Sunday morning. Peavine made his periodic immersions in country churches where the people didn't know that Peavine liked to be dipped and re-dipped just to be on the safe side. Tarp Davidson, the walking mailman, said, "That boy spends so much time in water it's a wonder he don't swivel up."

Salvation had been worrying Tommy Earl even before Leland Eugene Schmitt told him all about sex. Gene was four years older than his brother Neil and five years older than Tommy Earl. Gene Schmitt knew all about sex. He had learned some of it from Lonnie Maubry, a black kid who worked at Roy Rogers's filling station, some from a dirty eight-page comic book featuring Maggie and Jiggs that he found under his parents' bed, and some from a bunch of ninth graders who had grown up on the farm and knew all about sheep and other farm animals. Gene told Tommy Earl and Neil that sex was the most wonderful thing in the world and that you would burn in hell for it. You didn't have to do it, you just had to think about it to be damned forever. Since Neil and Tommy Earl were too young for the real thing, Gene warned against the kind you did by yourself. It would make you go blind at the worst and certainly cause you to grow hair in the palm of your hand. On the other hand, if you didn't do it at all, you would get acne all over your face. Gene told them about homosexuals, which surprised Tommy Earl since he had heard the word and thought homosexuals were people who did it at home.

Tommy Earl knew that hell gaped and was ready to snatch him off the earth any minute if he didn't get baptized like Peavine had done over and over. Tommy Earl's folks were Presbyterians, and Presbyterians, like the Methodists, didn't sink people completely under the water to save them from hell. Grady Dell used to tell the tale about some kids up near Telephone who tried to baptize a goat, but they couldn't get him to stand still in the creek long enough to dunk him. So one of the boys said, "Why don't we just sprinkle him the way the Methodists do and let him go on to hell." The Dells were not especially religious. Granny Dell and Tommy's Uncle Henry and Aunt Flora went to church about twice a month, and they made several revivals in the summer when Henry had laid his crops by. But the Dells, at least two generations of them, were not fanatical about church. Only Tommy Earl showed signs of serious Bible thumping, and that was because he saw the fine dash that Peavine Deerfield cut among the church ladies of Bodark Springs. And he had heard enough hellfire preachers describe the torments of hell to get as scared as Peavine must have been.

Anytime a church in Bodark Springs or anywhere in Eastis County, Texas, had a revival, Peavine was there, ready to make his way down the aisle when the call came for sinners to repent. Peavine went down and confessed his many and manifold sins, cried and snuffled a good deal, got patted on the head by all the old women along the aisle as he made his way down, and then was praised to high heaven by whatever preacher had opened the doors of the church as they were singing "Just as I am, without one plea." All this sanctity on Peavine's part made Tommy Earl nervous, made him wonder about his own sins, but he was way too scared to answer the altar call when he went to revivals.

Peavine was a star when the Holy Rollers had a tent meeting at the vacant lot behind Ralph Powers's cafe. The Holy Rollers had a mourners' bench down front, and the saved could hunker down on it and fall to wailing and taking on. Tommy Earl's parents didn't approve of all the church going he had been doing lately, and they sure didn't want him going to the Holy Rollers when they set up the tent. But one late July, when the temperature in East Texas was up near a hundred even at sunset, the Holy Rollers threw the biggest tent meeting Bodark Springs had seen since Hoover was president. Preacher Billy Mac Sanders had somehow got hold of a used, beat-up old carnival tent, the biggest ever seen in Bodark, and he had pitched it behind the cafe for the whole town to marvel at. Brother Sanders wanted to save the whole town in one short week. Tommy Earl and Fred Hallmark slipped off one night after their folks had gone to bed and went down to the tent about thirty minutes before the meeting broke up. They hid out behind Mr. Lawrence Armstrong's 1936 Dodge pickup, which was parked up near the mourners' bench. Mr. Armstrong and old man Israel Standifer had a couple of funeral parlor folding chairs between the truck and the edge of the tent, which had all the flaps up to let in the hot Texas wind. Neither Mr. Armstrong nor old man Standifer was religious, but they both loved a show. Lots of people in Bodark Springs went to the tent meetings to hear folks talk in tongues and grab for the Holy Ghost. One night about half way through the week's revival, old Calvin Cobb, who later died of food poisoning after eating out of the garbage cans behind C.C. Reed's grocery store, ran out of the tent and threw himself into a Model A Ford trying to grab the Holy Ghost. Of course, Calvin was drunk at the time, but Preacher Sanders saw it as a good sign that Calvin had got the spirit even though he broke an arm and knocked one of the parking lights off Earl McBrier's 1931 A-Model Ford.

Tommy Earl and Fred got to the tent revival in time to see Peavine Deerfield rush the mourners' bench and give his heart to God yet again. Peavine was down there before Preacher Sanders had had time to talk in tongues or fall on his own knees on the bench. When the preacher finally issued the call, one care-worn grass widow from Windom over in Fannin County ran down the aisle and threw herself half over the mourners' bench. Her dress flew up over her head, and Mrs. Gladys Lundy, the Avon lady, reached up to cover the widow's nether regions, but the preacher held up his hands and said, "No, Sister Lundy, leave her lay where Jesus flang her." And they did. Mr. Lawrence and Mr. Israel had to quickly put handkerchiefs over their mouths to keep from laughing out loud. Then old man Israel Standifer put on his glasses and looked hard at the widow woman spread eagled on the mourners' bench. He wasn't sure who she was, but he thought she might be from Honey Grove. He turned to Mr. Lawrence and said, "Is that Mother Green?" Mr. Lawrence looked over his dime-store glasses and said, "No, Israel, I think it was just the way the light hit it." Tommy Earl and Fred Hallmark ran all the way home talking about the widow woman's underwear.

After the crops were laid by in August, religion really got fired up in the country churches. There were protracted meetings, as the country people called revivals, and singing schools at the church houses, and serious saving and baptizing all over Fannin, Eastis, Grayson, and Lamar Counties, and no telling what all took place across the Red River in Oklahoma. Even the Choctaws got religion come August. Once, just over the river in Iron Stob, Oklahoma, a half-literate, jackleg preacher from down near Savoy saved and baptized a hundred people in one week of preaching. That was a record that got in newspapers all the way from Sherman to Texarkana.

Tommy Earl always spent two weeks in August with his Granny Dell and his Uncle Henry and Aunt Flora Irene. They had a daughter, Betty, who was five years older than Tommy Earl and had been saved at a Baptist revival a year or two back, even though all the Dells were Presbyterians. Her folks didn't like her making a spectacle of herself in front of a bunch of foot washers, but she broke away from her Granny Dell and ran down the aisle as they were singing "Almost Persuaded." Like the rest of the faithful, she took to hollering about Jesus and how she was saved. Henry and Flora Irene hated her cutting a dido like she did. They thought Presbyterians ought to know better than to get saved. Presbyterians were either going to heaven or hell. That had been decided when God created the world, so either you were or you weren't. That was all there was to say about that. At least that is what Henry told Betty after it was done. She got saved, but she didn't get baptized. She hadn't even been sprinkled the summer Tommy Earl came to stay with them. That was the summer Tommy was determined to go down at the altar call like Peavine always did. He didn't care if he was a Presbyterian.

Like most country people, Flora Irene and Henry made revivals all up and down the country backroads. It didn't matter—Baptist, Methodist, Holy Roller. It was the custom, and it had been observed in Eastis County since just after the Civil War. Now, here we were in the twentieth century, and still nothing was as edifying as good preaching, no matter what the godless Russian Communists or the Nazi Germans or the Catholic Italians might say. Everybody knew war was coming, and most thought religion was an answer to death and destruction.

In the middle of August, Flora Irene, Henry, Betty, and Tommy Earl loaded up in Henry's 1933 Chevrolet, the one he had bought from the old-maid schoolteachers Della and Alta Lee. Like his brother Grady, Henry always kept the car backed up on the hill beside the house, so he could let it roll down and start on compression when he popped the clutch. That saved what little battery he had left. He usually had enough battery to start the car when the meeting was over and get back home. On the way back, just about the time they crossed the O'Barr bridge, the old Chevy's lights began to dim and Henry always wondered if he could make it home in time to back up the hill before the battery played out.

The revival in mid-August was being held at the Mount Hebron Baptist Church out by the T&P tracks. Jim Stalnaker, the most famous Sacred Harp singing-school teacher in the county, was going to lead the singing, and Brother Hershel

Templeton from over at Honey Grove was doing the preaching. Brother Templeton had saved more souls in East Texas than anybody except Brother Sanders, the Holy Roller. Brother Templeton had saved Peavine Deerfield several times, but since he was such a soul saver, he didn't recognize the boy when he came down from one altar call to another.

The Mount Hebron church didn't have electricity, so along each side wall was a series of gas lanterns with little glowing sacks inside them and big reflectors on the back of each one. They didn't give out much light, but they put off enough heat to keep the congregation in mind of hell.

It had been a slow week for Brother Templeton in the soul-saving business. He hadn't collected enough offering money to pay for the gas he had burned up driving over from Honey Grove night after night. On this last night he purely meant to save some souls and raise some money. The church house was full, but the crowd seemed torpid. He fell to some of his hardest bound-to-save preaching. He promised them that they would have a "Glory Hallelujah Jubilee." But the heat and the weariness of the congregation was wearing him out. He got madder and madder until he finally told the crowd that they had failed him and failed God. He said, "Every night when that there T&P train rolls by this church house, old Satan hisself leans out of one of them freight cars and says, 'Y'all doin' fine, just fine.' Now tonight let's make a liar out of that old train-ridin' devil and prove to him that we won't be fine till we take the Holy Ghost into our hearts."

He didn't get much response, but he said, "Instead of the usual invitational hymn, I am going to get Brother Stalnaker to lead us in that fine old gospel song that has saved many a soul, and I am going to open the doors of the church and ask you to come down here and give your hearts to God when we sing "When They Ring Those Golden Bells." It's number 226 in your Harvest Hymns, a songbook published right here in Texas. Right down in Dallas by Brother Coleman."

Peavine was off like a shot before Jim Stalnaker rose to his feet. Brother Templeton said, "Hold on a minute, boy, I ain't ready to open the doors of the church yet. You will get your chance to come down here and witness to these good people. All right, Brother Stalnaker." Down by the mourners' bench Old Jim Stalnaker rose up and began talking out the song:

> There's a land beyond the river
> That we call the sweet forever.
> And we only reach that shore by faith's decree.
> One by one we'll gain the portals,
> There to dwell with the immortals.
> "Now sing with me," Brother Stalnaker said,
> When they ring those golden bells for you and me,
> When they ring those bells, when they ring those bells,
> It's a glory hallelujah jubilee.

Then suddenly there was a loud bang, like somebody had pulled both triggers on a twelve-gauge shotgun. The women screamed, and six or seven men pulled great long pistols out from under their suit coats and whirled toward the sound.

Brother Templeton said, "Goddam you men! Put them guns away! It was just one of them Coleman lanterns that blowed up. I never seen the like of you people. Pulling guns here in the house of the Lord!" Then the preacher fell to his knees and lifted up his head and said, "Forgive me, Lord. I takened your name in vain. But I was drove to it by these heathens bringing guns into your house. That old devil that rides the T&P may be right. We don't deserve to be saved."

Tommy Earl had ducked back behind his Aunt Flora Irene when the lamp blew up and didn't hear the preacher take the Lord's name in vain. He did see Emily Stringer faint and fall against her mother. Then he cried out to his aunt, "Aunt 'Rene look yonder at Mrs. Pearl Farley! She looks like she is about to faint and fall out!"

Flora Irene turned to Henry and said, "Quick! Grab Pearl Farley. She is about to fall your way!"

And Pearl did. Right out in the aisle. Too quick for Henry or anybody else to catch her. It sounded like somebody had dropped a two-by-twelve. Old pussel-gutted Lee Cline bent to pick her up, but she was too much for him. It took Lee Cline and Henry and finally her husband Cleatis to half drag her back to her seat. Three or four women began fanning her with the fans T. B. Whitmire's funeral parlor and furniture store always provided churches. Pearl came to and said, "Did anybody shoot that preacher? They should have. Did you hear him talking ugly up there in that pulpit?"

Nobody had shot the preacher, and nobody else fainted. But a real damper had been put on the revival, and there was no chance of a great soul saving on this last night. The preacher tried to carry on and told Jim Stalnaker to finish the gospel song that he had started. It was not going to help, but Stalnaker sadly and mournfully finished up:

> In that far off sweet forever,
> Just beyond the shining river,
> When they ring those golden bells for you and me.

But it was all over at the Mount Hebron Baptist Church. It was all over for Tommy Earl Dell, who had moved out into the aisle during the singing. He had meant to make that long walk to the mourners' bench, but now he slid back in the pew next to his cousin Betty. He whispered to her, "What's a glory hallelujah jubilee?"

Betty had learned to cuss that summer, so she whispered back, "Damned if I know, but that sure as hell wasn't one." And then all the Dells eased out of the church house and loaded up in Henry's 1933 Chevrolet and hoped they could make it home before the battery gave plumb out and they had to get on home in total darkness.

Tommy Earl never managed to get "saved," and Betty backslid into the staid Presbyterianism of her forbears. Peavine testified right up to the time that war broke out, and then he completely lost his religion for the duration. Tommy Earl Dell drifted from Presbyterianism to Methodism as he grew up. Long after he left Bodark Springs and moved to Fort Worth, he met a woman who was the daughter of an Episcopal clergyman. They didn't marry, but Tommy—he was now Tom or T. E. Dell—got baptized and confirmed in the Protestant Episcopal Church of the United States. After several years of allegiance to The Thirty-Nine Articles, Tom E. Dell decided that the best course for a man of his skepticism was the Unitarian Church.

Once, back in Bodark Springs for "Foots" Waller's funeral, the Reverend J. William Deerfield (aka Peavine) asked Tom Dell if he had ever got saved. Tom said he had not even fallen on the mourners' bench and rolled around on the floor, but he had become "churched" after he left Bodark Springs.

"What are you? You a Methodist or something?"

"No, Reverend Peavine, I am a member of the Unitarian/ Universalist congregation."

"Well, you know what they say about Unitarians, don't you? They believe in one God—at most."

Mr. T. E. Dell smiled and allowed that he didn't need religious instructions from a member of the Free Jesus Holy Name Holiness Church of Bodark Springs, Texas.

ELEVEN

Rock-Ola

1941

Mrs. Pearl Farley was talking to her husband Cleatis. It was Friday night, payday night, in Eastis County, Texas, and Mrs. Farley was frying a piece a round steak, the first meat they had had since Tuesday. Cleatis sat at the kitchen table watching her. Pearl said, over her shoulder, "Every slut and whoremonger in Eastis County is gonna be up at that-there Moon River Beach whiskey house when it opens tomorrow night."

This minor outburst caught Cleatis by surprise. He had told Pearl about the new honky-tonk's grand opening nearly an hour ago and she hadn't said a word. Now he knew that—once again—he should have kept his mouth shut. He didn't know what to say, so he ducked his head and said, "Well, Pearlie, I guess they will be people there from Fannin and Lamar counties—and probably some from over in Oklahoma if the ferry is still running after all this rain."

"Don't you Pearlie me, Cleatis Farley. I know you wish you was going."

Cleatis not only wished it, but he had a plan to be there as soon as the doors opened.

Feeling guilty about the elaborate lies he would have to tell to make the grand opening, Cleatis blushed and said, "Me, no, I don—"

Pearl wheeled around from the stove, waving the skillet full of meat and gravy at Cleatis, and said, "Well, you can just forget it, Mr. Cleatis L. Farley. I know what you think, but I don't aim to be married to no sot drunkard, so don't let it cross your mind again. Do you hear me? You ain't ever going up there. Don't you ever even mention that honky-tonk to me again. Well, I mean, Lord God Almighty—the Moon River Beach!"

Cleatis never mentioned the Moon River Beach again—at least not to Pearl. But she was right: every slut and whoremonger and cotton chopper and tie hacker and coal miner and ironworker and round dancer in three counties and part of Oklahoma showed up. And had a good time.

Even Cleatis L. Farley. Cleatis got Old Man Mike Sharpe to let him take Jim Bagwell's place and haul a big load of lumber over to Denison, then across the bridge to Durant, and back east toward Bokchita. A trip like that would take all day Saturday. Then Cleatis planned a breakdown once he got back across the Red into Texas and turned east toward the Moon River Beach.

Everybody had a good time but Grady Dell, the rural letter carrier from Bodark Springs. And his wife Mamie. And maybe Grady's nephew J. T. and J. T.'s wife Hattie. They all had to leave the grand opening early.

Mamie had been getting ready for a week or so for the Saturday night that Clyde and Meridian Wilson unveiled the finest roadhouse in Northeast Texas in that fall of 1941 when, though Eastis County didn't know it, it was drifting with the rest of Texas and the world toward Pearl Harbor.

On the Monday before the grand opening, Mamie Dell told Dr. Clayton's nurse, Emily Stringer, "I gonna dance my shoe heels as round as apples on Saturday night up at Clyde and

Meridian's new place. What about you, Emily? Are you planning to go?"

That was a mean thing to say because Emily, the woman that Grady always called "that little old narrow-assed girl of Bud Stringer's," hadn't had a date in two years, and everybody in Bodark knew it. She hadn't danced a step since Roy Amos went off to join the CCC camps and never came back. Emily always used to look wistful and said, "Nobody ever knew where Roy wound up."

Emily, who needed to gain at least twenty pounds to get up to Bodark Springs courting weight, smoothed down the white paper on the examining table as Mamie sat in the chair waiting for Dr. Clayton. Emily looked over at Mamie and said, "I don't guess anybody'll ask me, but I sure would like to go up there. If nothing else just to see that place."

Mamie had come in to see to Dr. Clayton about her gall bladder. Mamie Dell was the only person in Bodark Springs except for Dr. Clayton who knew exactly where the gall bladder was located. And how one felt if it got out of whack—Mamie told Doshie McBrier once, "The first time my gall bladder went out, hon, all my muscles locked up on me—all the way from my waist up to my shoulders."

Mamie knew visceral organs. She knew more about a person's insides than old Dr. Elgin, the town's other doctor, and nearly as much as Dr. Clayton. Mamie had good reason to be an expert in the medical arts and sciences. She had overcome liver cancer without medical help, had suffered shooting pains in her back, "jumping headaches," clogged sinuses, a misfunctioning spleen, more heart flutters than she could count, both low and high blood pressure, rheumatism, bursitis in both shoulders, tonsillitis, impacted wisdom teeth—the worst Dr. Powers had ever seen, Mamie always said—spastic colon, some female problems still not reported in the medical literature, and a bad case of pernicious anemia. Mamie bragged that by the age of thirty she had had seven major operations and two of the hardest births ever witnessed in Eastis County, Texas. But no matter how bad the pain was all day—and often in the dark hours of the morning—Mamie always got well enough to go honky-tonking when whippoorwills called and evening was nigh. And she always, as she said, "danced her shoeheels as round as apples."

Emily said, "You've been up to the Moon River Beach, haven't you, Mamie?"

"Oh, Lord God yes, hon, lots of times. Me and Grady nearly built that place we was up there so much. Our daughter—you know Jackie don't you?—well did you know she named the Moon River Beach? Don't you think that's the prettiest name you ever heard? We are close friends to Clyde and Meridian, so we started going up there to see how the place was coming along as soon as they had Leon Cogburn in to grade off the land. Moon River Beach. Clyde wanted to call it Clyde's Place, but Meridian wouldn't have none of that. She wanted to call it the Coconut Grove after that one up in Boston that you hear about on the radio, but when she went to see Madame Ora Lee to have her and Clyde's fortune told, Madame Ora Lee told her not to name it the Coconut Grove because it would be bad luck. Well, anyway, we was up there once and Jackie looked off the bluff and said, 'Why don't y'all call it the Moon River Beach?' Well, Clyde, he looked down at the Red River, down where all them cottonmouth moccasins live at and like to of puked. I mean he didn't like that name. But Meridian did, and you know who wears the pants in that family. So Meridian told Clyde to call Boyd McLaughlin and get him to paint a sign with a moon on it and have it say Moon River Beach."

Emily waited patiently till Mamie paused for breath, then asked, "Have they got anything good to dance to on the Rock-Ola?"

Mamie said, "Oh, Lord God, hon, they've got everything. That Rock-Ola holds twelve records, and except for two that Meridian wants on there—and I don't know why—they are all fine dance music. They got Lulu Bell and Scottie singing 'Remember Me'—that song that Grady is so crazy about. He won't go near a music machine that don't have 'Remember Me' on it. I'm getting tired of it myself, but I swear I think Grady would play it every time if he was the only one putting nickels in the coin slide. But then I'm glad to say he ain't. And they got that new Ernest Tubbs record 'I'm Walking the Floor Over You,' and another new one 'When My Blue Moon Turns to Gold Again.' Have you heard that song, Emily?"

Emily had, but had never danced to it, and so she didn't exactly consider that she had really heard it. And though she hadn't yet danced to the song, she at least knew that Ernest's name wasn't Tubbs but just Tubb and that the right title was "Walking the Floor Over You." Emily knew a lot more about what songs were popular than Mamie did, but she hadn't had the first-hand, honky-tonk experience that made Mamie an expert on high life in East Texas.

Mamie went on, "Oh, and they've got Gene Autry singing 'That Silver-haired Daddy of Mine'—don't you just love that song?—and somebody singing Hattie's favorite song, 'Maple on the Hill.'"

Emily asked Mamie, "Is it Mainer's Mountaineers?"

"Is what Mainer's Mountaineers?"

"That's singing 'Maple on the Hill'?"

Mamie looked piteously at Emily and said, "Oh, honey, I don't pay no attention to who sings them if it ain't some big star like Gene Autry or Ernest Tubbs." She couldn't resist another dig at poor, dateless Emily and said, "See I'm usually so busy dancing that I don't read what's written on the Rock-Ola and somebody else always puts the nickels in anyway. Now, let's see, there's 'It Makes no Difference Now'—God, I love that song." And Mamie sang a snatch of it:

> Makes no difference now what kind of life they hand me,
> I'll get along somehow you know it's plain to see.

"That sure tells my story, Emily. And they've got 'Nobody's Darling But Mine' and another one by Gene Autry—'Tears on My Pillow.' How many is that?"

"That's eight. Have they got Bob Wills's song 'New San Antonio Rose'?"

"Well, they got 'San Antonio Rose,' but I don't know about 'New.' Oh, and there's 'You're the Only Star in My Blue Heaven.' That's all of them, right?"

"Well, except for them other two you mentioned. You know, the ones that Meridian put on the Rock-Ola, that you don't like."

"Yeah, well, you know, they are songs you hear on the radio all the time. One of them is 'Stardust,' and the other one is that theme song that they play on the radio ever day when Tommy Dorsey comes on."

"'I'm Getting Sentimental Over You.'"

Mamie looked up sharply, "What? What did you say?"

Emily blushed, "That song. You know, Tommy Dorsey's theme song, 'I'm Getting Sentimental Over You.'"

"Oh, yeah, right, I guess that is the title. Well, anyway, they have got some good songs on that Rock-Ola. I just wish they had more."

Emily said, "You know I have heard that there is a music machine over in Sherman that has twenty-four songs on it. But I haven't ever seen it."

Mamie seemed startled by this piece of news. "Twenty-four songs? I don't know where they put the records. Must be some new kind of Rock-Ola."

Mamie was still talking about music when Dr. Clayton came into the room, but she shut up quickly and began laying a trap for her internal organs.

By Saturday, all the sluts and whoremongers and heavy drinkers and round dancers had worked themselves to a fever pitch. Grady Dell had finished his mail route and was checking out his money orders as he thought about the Moon River Beach. He and Mamie were going with his nephew J. T. and J. T.'s wife, Hattie. J. T. was Grady's brother's boy, but he had always been closer to Grady than to his own father. J. T. had been running whiskey all through the Depression and had only lately taken over the boat landing up the river from the Moon River Beach and just across from Iron Stob, Oklahoma. J. T. sold a few cans of sardines a week, rented a few boats, and handled a good bit of bootleg whiskey. What he didn't sell, he drank. People in Eastis County used to mention J. T.'s drinking in hushed tones. They would look serious and say, "Well, you know, J. T., he dranks." The tone and language meant that J. T. was putting away about a quart of whiskey a day. And had been for twenty years. Homer Brantley once said to Grady, "J. T. ain't drawed a sober breath in twenty years." Grady might have hit anybody else who had said this, but Homer Brantley was a one-armed man, so Grady just turned and walked off.

Grady was looking forward to Saturday night at the Moon River Beach. He didn't have much excitement in his life. Mamie was always sick, they got in debt and lost their house in 1936, and Grady had had a stroke in '38 and spent nearly six months in the VA hospital in Waco. He didn't see much to look forward to. Jackie and Tommie Earl were good children, but Jackie would get married any time now and Grady was forty years older than Tommy Earl, so the boy seemed more like a grandson than a son and Grady doubted that he would ever live to see him grown.

A few years ago, on his way to George Moore's Cafe for a couple of bottles of beer before going home, Grady decided that he hadn't ever had but two good years in his life. The rest of his fifty years had been as dull as today. But back in 1917, he had been drafted into the army, given six weeks training at Camp Pike, Arkansas, put on the train for Fort Dix, New Jersey, and then on a ship for Europe to serve in the American Expeditionary Forces.

Grady's outfit, the 18th Infantry of the First Division, went into the Argonne led by a colonel. They came out led by a corporal. More than a thousand lay dead among the stumps of what had once been a great forest.

After the war was over, Grady spent nine months in the Army of Occupation in Koblenz. They quartered him on a German family named Gerber, and he fell in love with their second daughter Eva, who loved him back. Grady would have stayed in Germany if the Gerbers hadn't forced Eva to live up to her marriage contract to a butcher from Cologne. Maybe because he really loved her, or maybe because she was so suddenly snatched away from him, Grady always thought of Eva Gerber as the great love of his life.

The night before she was to leave for Cologne, she and Grady met at midnight in the outbuilding behind Gerber's house and made love. Eva cried and sang a few verses of an old German folksong, "Vergisst mein nicht." Grady asked what it meant and she said, "It means that I don't want you to forget me. Forget me nicht. 'Remember me,' I guess you would say. Will you, Grady?"

"Oh, Eva, I'll always remember you. And I'll always love you, too," Grady said, and sobbed.

And he always had. Sometimes he remembered Eva in the strangest places.

That Saturday night at the Moon River Beach was one of them.

J. T. and Hattie came to get Mamie and Grady in J. T.'s uncle Ev Crider's 1936 Buick, borrowed because J. T.'s 1937 Ford 60 had blown a head gasket. Everybody always said J. T. drove so fast that he was likely to melt the spindles off a car. He hadn't melted the spindles, but he had blown the head gasket off what he called "that worst goddamned Ford that Henry ever made. It won't pull the hat off your goddamned head." And since J. T. and Hattie both weighed about two hundred fifty pounds apiece, it was good luck that J. T. had Ev Crider's Buick, because J. T.'s Ford 60 would never have hauled them all up Butts Hill, and Grady's beat-up 1938 Chevy had the back seats out so he could haul the Sears catalogs twice a year and all the orders of baby chicks that came in the mail nearly every day.

J. T., red in the face, wearing a half-cast/half-bandage on his left hand where Dr. Clayton had cut a wen off, had nearly a full tank of whiskey in him when he wheeled Ev Crider's blue '36 Buick up to the front door of the Moon River Beach. The parking lot was nearly full, but Clyde had thrown Boyd McLaughlin out for trying to whip Edward Hurst, and Boyd had vacated a space right next to the front door.

"I-God, they knowed to save one for me," J. T. said as he nearly rammed Burt Moore's '36 Chevrolet Master Deluxe that was parked in the next space.

Inside, the din was heartening to Grady. The Rock-Ola was playing "When My Blue Moon Turns to Gold Again," so he took Mamie on a turn around the dance floor before they even tried to find a seat. When the song was over and Ernest Tubb started singing "Walking the Floor over You," J. T. had got a table for four right up near where the dance hall part of the honky-tonk joined the barroom. Up near where the waitresses picked up orders and where people went to whisper to Ed Butts to run outside and get them a half pint of whiskey. Ed, the best barbecue man in East Texas, had been stolen by Clyde from a joint over near Bogota where Ed was cooking for a dollar a day and selling whiskey on the halves. At the Moon River Beach, Ed cooked free but had the bootlegging concession all to himself. On Friday nights, about dark, Ed began hiding half pints all around the back half acre of the Moon River Beach. He put them under slabs left over from the construction, under barrels that had once held coal oil, and all along the back side of the five tourist court cabins that Clyde had built in case anybody at the Moon River Beach met somebody nice and needed somewhere to go.

J. T. had already asked Ed to get him a half pint by the time Grady caught Ed going out the back door and ordered his own half pint. Grady had already had several drinks out of the half pint that J. T. had brought from the boat landing, and he had had three beers at Ralph Powers's cafe on the way home from work. By now, he was not sober, but he was not drunk. He was just right. Or maybe just half a step past right.

When he had placed his order with Ed Butts, he headed toward the table where Mamie and Hattie and J. T. were settling in for a night of it. Half way across the floor, he saw Mamie jump up from where she was sitting and say in a loud voice, "You get the hell away from me, you bastard! Don't you touch me or I'll bust your head open with this Co-Cola bottle!"

The man Mamie was shouting at was a stranger to Grady, but he could tell at a glance that he must be one of the ironworkers helping build the ammunition plant up near Valliant, Oklahoma. Grady could see a table of ironworkers standing up and laughing at Mamie hollering at the man, a man who looked amazingly like that goddamned fat butcher from Cologne, Germany. The man laughed and grabbed at Mamie's arm again.

As Grady got to the table, Lulu Belle and Scottie started singing "Remember Me" on the Rock-Ola. Suddenly Grady saw Eva's butcher husband as plain as day. He saw Eva Gerber. And he saw the sorry life he was living now, a life that was beginning to shut down all around him. He hardly noticed that he had the ironworker by the shirt collar and his right hand drawn back to hit "that goddamn German butcher." Grady came to himself when J. T. grabbed his arm and said, "Let me hit that sumbitch, Un' Grady. You too old to fight."

Grady shook J. T. off and heard himself saying, as if in a dream, "By God, it looks like this place needs cleaning out. You wanta help me out?"

J. T., blustering and strutting, said, "You damn right. You goddamned right. I been wantin to try this goddam cast out on somebody's head. Where you wanna start?"

Grady still held the ironworker by the collar. He looked around and said, "With the first son of a bitch that opens his mouth."

Mamie, who had been caught up in the excitement, froze. Hattie thought, if I didn't weigh so much I might just get under this table. Cleatis Farley, who had called his next-door neighbor and got her to tell Pearl that he was "broke down up between Blue and Bochita," reached his brogan over and kicked the Rock-Ola plug out of the wall just as Ed Butts flipped the switch that turned on every light in the place.

Grady stood, still holding the ironworker by the collar. The ironworker looked dazed but not the least bit afraid. Ed Butts stepped away from the fuse box and set two half pints of bootleg under the counter. Clyde Wilson was scrabbling around behind the beer box trying to get his Browning double-barrel twelve gauge. Just in case. Nobody in the house moved or said a word as J. T. and Grady looked all around the dance hall. Far off in the kitchen, one of the cooks had the Paris radio station—KPLT—turned on low; Grady could hear it plain. It was playing "Remember Me."

Grady said, "Well, Goddamn!" and turned the ironworker's shirt collar loose. He turned to J. T. and said, "Jate, if these bastards are too scared to fight, let's go somewhere else." He turned to Mamie and Hattie and said, "Y'all coming?"

By this time J. T. was starting to draw his first sober breath in twenty years. Or was afraid he was. Mamie picked up Grady's hat, got her purse from the chair that was pushed under the table, and motioned for Hattie to move. Hattie was frozen, and Mamie had to shake her by the arm to get her even to blink. Then the four of them backed out of the dance hall, backed across the bar room next to it, backed out the door—Grady last—and got into Ev Crider's 1936 Buick.

J. T., still looking at the front door, said, "I-God, I hope this sumbitch will start. I hope to God this sumbitch will start."

When it did, J. T. put in the clutch, shifted into reverse, and eased out into the parking lot. Just then the lights on the dance floor went off and somebody plugged the Rock-Ola back in. The record, still resting in the circle that slid the records off the pile, started turning and the needle fell back into place with a hum as Lulu Belle and Scottie started "Remember Me" from where they had left off when Cleatis jerked the plug out.

By now, J. T. had calmed down some. He turned to Grady and said, "We coulda whipped them sumbitches. You wanta go back in there?"

Grady had the Buick's window down and was listening to the song as it floated out through the open windows of the Moon River Beach. And thinking of the only exciting years he had ever had. He took a long time to answer. Finally, he turned to J. T. and said, "Naw, let's leave it with them and go on home."

As they rolled off the lot, Grady could hear Lulu Belle and Scotty singing:

> The sweetest words belong to lovers in the gloaming
> The sweetest days are the days that used to be
> The saddest words I ever heard were words of parting
> When you said "Sweetheart, remember me."

TWELVE

Navy Blue and Gold

1944

In the spring of 1944, the courthouse square in Bodark Springs, Texas, looked almost exactly the way it had during World War I. For that matter, it wasn't much changed from the days of the Spanish-American War fifty years before. Of course there hadn't been any cars parked around the square in 1898, and the courthouse, being only ten years old, still looked new. But there weren't many cars on the square now. Gas was rationed, and most people's tires were rags in this, the third year of the war. People mostly walked in town, and if they traveled, they were likely to ride the train or bus to Sherman and catch the Interurban trolley to Dallas.

The square gleamed under one of those clear, brilliant days that come to East Texas between rains and thunderstorms and tornadoes in the spring. Tommy Earl Dell and Fred Hallmark had just got out of school. They sat on their bikes on the sidewalk in front of the Texas Power and Light Company office looking at the pictures of soldiers and sailors that filled both storefront windows of the power company.

"I can't wait to join up," Tommy Earl said. And he sighed.

Fred joined the sigh and said, "Me neither. If they whip Hitler and Hirohito before we turn seventeen, we are going to miss the whole war. And I'd hate that because my brother Ben always writes home about how much fun he's having."

"Where's he at?" asked Tommy Earl, who had just turned thirteen and imagined himself defending Wake Island or being dug in on the beach at Guadalcanal.

Fred, six months older and therefore half a year closer to going to war, turned from staring at Ben's picture and said, "They won't let him say, but Momma thinks he might be in England. He keeps talking about rain and fog in his letters."

"Boy, I can't wait to join up. I may go marine. But then I have thought about joining the navy and learning a trade. That's how Joe McBrier learned to be a machinist. In the navy back in nineteen and eighteen," Tommy Earl said.

Then he added, "My daddy said if he could go again, he'd still go in the army. He says you always have the ground under your feet and can fall down if they start to shoot. He was in the First Division in First World War. Did I tell you that?"

"About a million times."

"Screw you."

"Screw you, too. And screw your daddy."

"How would you like me to knock you on your ass?"

"How would you like to try?"

Both boys had stomped down their kickstands and were climbing off their bikes when Mrs. Bertha Lawler came out of the power company and stopped to look back at her son Lewis's picture up on the Gold Star shelf. The boys froze as Mrs. Lawler, who had taught both of them in the sixth grade, looked at the photo of her dead son.

She turned to them and said, "Hello boys, are you all admiring our soldiers and sailors?"

"Yessum," they both said at once. They couldn't think of

anything to say, knowing that she was looking at the picture of her son who died when the *USS Houston* went down two years before. Lewis Lawler was the third boy from Bodark Springs to die in the war. James Walker died on the *Oklahoma* at Pearl Harbor and Raymond Byers was killed at Corregidor. Now, in the spring of 1944, there were twenty-six boys from Eastis County on the Gold Star shelf in the power company's window.

"Did you boys know that the power company started putting up these pictures as soon as they started drafting the boys for service in 1940?"

"Nome," they both said. But they knew. They knew more about the photos in the window than Mrs. Lawler did. Fred and Tommy Earl spent an hour or two a week looking in the windows and dreaming about being fighters against Hitler and Tojo. Either boy could have told you exactly where every picture was in the window and what kind of frame everybody's picture was in. Most of the eight-by-ten frames with gold edging had come from the Ben Franklin store on the square. The proud mothers tore out the pictures of Tyrone Power or Madge Evans or Ronald Reagan that came with the frames and put in photos of their own boys. By 1944, some of the "boys" were girls. Emma Martin had joined the WAVES as soon as she finished high school, and Mrs. Ruth Foster, whose husband had died in training at Randolph Field, was now training to be a flyer herself out at Sweetwater. Altogether, there were seven girls from Eastis County in the armed services.

"Did you know they's a nigger girl's picture up in the power company window?" Fred had said to Tommy Earl one day in school.

"She's colored," Tommy Earl angrily. "Anybody willing to join up ain't a nigger. She's colored. I ain't seen you running down to sign up."

"Well, I will. Just as soon as I turn seventeen."

Tommy Earl, who was half a head taller than Fred Hallmark, said, "Well, I'm gonna lie about my age when I get to five-seven, and I'm gonna join the Marine Corps."

"Shit, you'll be right here in Bodark Springs when the war's over. They wouldn't have you in the marines. Army either. You'll get the same thing your daddy got when he tried to join up last year. They'll throw you out on your ass."

Tommy Earl's clumsy haymaker hit Fred just above the right ear. They rolled around the floor of Mrs. Lawler's class until she broke them up. That had happened two years before, but Mrs. Lawler hadn't forgotten.

She said, "Is fighting all you boys ever think about? You looked like you were about to start when I came out the door."

"Nome, we don't fight much," Tommy Earl said, "but sometimes Fred says things just to devil me."

"Me? Me! I ain't the one that starts—"

"Don't say 'ain't,' Freddy," Mrs. Lawler said in her sixth-grade tone.

"Nome, I won't, but Tommy Earl ain't—idn't—telling the truth. That's all."

Mrs. Lawler changed the subject. "I know you are proud of Ben off serving in the air corps, aren't you?"

"Yessum, all of us are. And I'm gonna join up and be a flyer, too, just like your boy Charles there."

The three of them turned to look back at the window and saw Charles Lawler standing in front of a Navy Hellcat wearing a flight jacket and goggles. Charles was stationed on a carrier in the Pacific and had already won the Navy Cross. He was scheduled to come home before summer. Then he would be transferred to Coronado Island in San Diego to be an instructor. The plane Charles Lawler stood in front of had a boot and a map of Texas painted on the side. And, as any boy in Bodark Springs could tell you, the words "Red River Ranger" encircled the boot and map. Most of the schoolboys in Eastis County had decorated the backs of their school notebooks with drawings of Charles Lawler's plane.

Anytime Tommy Earl saw Charles's picture, he thought about James Stewart in the movie *Navy Blue and Gold.* It was Tommy's all-time favorite picture show. He had seen it once when his father took him to the Majestic in Dallas, and he sat through it twice when it came to the Pines Theater in Bodark Springs just before the war started.

"Well, you boys don't be too quick to join the services. It's a whole lot worse over there than they make it seem in the picture shows. Y'all think about that, you hear?"

"Yessum," they both said.

But neither one believed her. What could she know about the fighting? Her boy Lewis got killed, but that was in a sneak attack. Now that Americans had warning, it wasn't so easy to kill them.

"I don't care what she says," Fred said, "I'm joining up."

"Me, too. And I ain't gonna let no Jap slip up on me. I'll be watching."

Back in a good humor again, the boys parted as Fred rode off in the direction of the Hallmark Cafe where his father served the best food in Bodark Springs, ran the Greyhound bus station, and took care of Western Union Telegraph deliveries for Eastis County.

Fred helped out around the cafe and delivered telegrams on his bike unless one came in from the War or Navy Department. Then Mr. Hallmark went home, put on his suit and his dark tie, and carried the message that began "The War Department regrets to inform you" to the family. Twenty-six times in the past two years, John Ed Hallmark had had calls from Max McGlothin over at the T&P Station to "come on over and get a telegram from the govermint." Max never said who the wire was for, and

John Ed never asked. He simply took off his apron, told whoever was cooking that he would be back in an hour, went out and got in his brown '38 Chevrolet Tudor, and drove over to the T&P. Then he went home and changed. Mrs. Hallmark never asked who the message was for. John Ed never told her till he got back and changed out of his suit. Then he would say, "Mrs. Macon's boy Robert got killed in Italy," or "Mrs. Sampson's boy is missing over Germany."

Mrs. Hallmark always prayed when John Ed left. She prayed for the boy's soul. And for the mother. And then for the father of the soldier or sailor who was dead. Then she prayed for John Ed. Those twenty-six trips had nearly killed him. He never said anything, but she could see him shrinking more and more into himself with each telegram.

John Ed Hallmark's brown Chevy became known as the "Death Chariot." John Ed got to the point that he hated to drive the car to church or to the grocery store for fear that mothers and fathers of servicemen would quake when they saw the car come down their street. In the fall of 1943, Hallmark started leaving the car at home when he went to work, but that didn't solve anything. When anybody saw him leave the cafe in the middle of the day and start for home, they just had longer to wait and worry while he walked the ten blocks to his house to get changed and get the car out of the garage. So, in the winter, he began driving to work again. He figured that driving got the agony over quicker.

Each day that passed got to be a hell for John Ed Hallmark. His stomach tightened every time the phone rang at the cafe. And if the phone at home rang at night, John Ed, Mrs. Hallmark, and Fred sat up in their beds. Mrs. Hallmark prayed that the call wasn't about Ben. Then she prayed for forgiveness for wishing bad news—if it was bad news—on some other mother.

If the lights came on in the Hallmark house at night, the

neighbors seemed to know it. The next day, whispers went all over town.

"Did you see the lights come on last night at the Hallmarks' house?"

"Yeah, about eleven o'clock. I wonder who it was this time?"

John Ed knew how tense everybody was, so he trained himself to go to the bathroom without a light. Once night he snapped at Fred for turning on his light when the boy got sick and had to call his mother.

"Can't you leave that light off, boy?"

"Yessir, but I was about to throw up, and I had—"

That was as far as Fred got before he vomited all over the bed. John Ed reddened with shame for chastising the child.

While Fred Hallmark made his way toward the cafe to start his after-school chores, Tommy Earl walked his bike down the street toward the Bodark Cleaners where he worked part time after school and all day on Saturdays. He would have to carry dry cleaning all over town from now until five o'clock. If the paper bags with suits and dresses in them went to businesses or to houses close to the cleaners, Tommy Earl walked. If a few pieces had to be carried across town, he rode his bike and either hooked the coat hangers in his shirt collar or held them over his left shoulder and steered the bicycle with his right hand. If there was a big load to be carried, Smith McMasters, who owned the cleaners, drove the car and Tommy carried the clothes up to the door.

When Tommy Earl got to the cleaners, he found that he had six deliveries—all in different directions. He decided to save Mrs. Lawler's for last since she had three dresses, and he hated hauling dresses on his bike. Dresses were bagged in long paper sacks, and it was all he could do to keep the sacks—and sometimes the dresses—from getting tangled up in the spokes of the back wheel. He couldn't hang dresses on his shirt collar, so sometimes, if he had to go up a hill, he was forced to get off and walk, half pushing, half dragging the bike with one hand.

By four forty-five, Tommy Earl had delivered all but Mrs. Lawler's cleaning. He lifted the sacks high over his shoulder and set out down Jeff Davis Street and out toward the nicest part of Bodark Springs. Out by Dr. Clayton's two-story house and on out past where Thurman Whitmire the furniture dealer and undertaker lived. And old Doc Lowry, the chiropractor. And the town's three lawyers. And some other families who hadn't been ruined by the Depression.

He coasted past Dr. Clayton's house, admiring the 1939 La Salle "doctor's coupe" with its bullet-shaped lights that seemed to grow out of the hood. He almost ran out in front of John Ed Hallmark rolling slowly down Jeff Davis toward town.

"I wonder who he's killed now?" Tommy Earl said aloud as he saw Mr. Hallmark's white face wearing the look that everybody in Bodark knew by now. It was a face that reminded Tommy Earl of the Angel of Death in the Bible storybook that he used to look at in Sunday School. John Ed Hallmark was solemn and black-browed, but before the war, he had been a jolly, heavyset man with a red face. Now, he was pallid and his clothes hung on him.

One day, Ellie May Moore, who did alterations at the dry cleaners, said to Mrs. Estella Montgomery, "You know I bet John Ed Hallmark has lost fifty pounds since Pearl Harbor. I have took up these pants and that suit of his four times. Blamed if the back pockets don't nearly meet. If this war don't get over, he is gonna die from it."

When Tommy Earl got to Mrs. Lawler's house, he was relieved to see her standing on the front porch waiting for him. At least the death message wasn't about her son Charles who was coming home soon. Maybe Mr. Hallmark was delivering a regular telegram, or maybe his death message was for somebody out in the country and he was just coming back to town by way of

Jeff Davis Street.

Mrs. Lawler smiled at Tommy and said, "Come on up, Tommy Earl, and I'll write a check for my cleaning."

Tommy walked toward her, being careful to keep the dresses from dragging the ground. He smiled at her and said, "Oh, you don't need to give me a check now. Mr. McMasters will send your bill on the first of the month."

"Well, I may not be here on the first. Maybe you'd better take the check now," she said.

"School ain't out yet. You can't just up and go—"

"Don't say 'ain't,' son," she said in a way that didn't sound like a sixth-grade teacher.

She's never called me son before, Tommy thought.

"Yessum," he said, "aren't . . . I mean isn't. Yessum."

"Oh, it's all right this time," she said, "but try to remember."

"Yessum."

She wrote the check while Tommy waited. Then she handed it to him and did something so strange that Tommy stumbled back off the step: she leaned over and kissed him on the top of the head.

"Bye, Tommy Earl," she said, almost in a whisper.

"Yessum, uh, I mean, bye."

As he rode back toward the room he and his mother had been living in since his father's second stroke had put him in the veterans' hospital in Waco, Tommy Earl shook his head and wondered why Mrs. Lawler seemed so strange.

It was the next day before he heard that Mrs. Lawler went in the house, drew the shades in the front room, and reached a hand out from behind the shade to take down Charles's navy blue star that had hung beside Lewis's gold one for most of the war.

THIRTEEN

Home Front Heroes

1945

Tommy Earl Dell loved World War II.

So did Fred Hallmark, Hal Holley, J. T. Martin, and his tongue-tied brother Roy.

Every boy in the fifth and sixth grades at the Stonewall Jackson Elementary School in Bodark Springs, Texas, loved World War II.

Even Peavine Deerfield, who quit getting "saved" when Roosevelt declared war on the Imperial Japanese government the day after Pearl Harbor, gave up religion in favor of patriotism. He said, "I'd kill every damn Jap and German there is—and them Eye-talians, too."

Ellie Pearl Walker, who weighed in at 160 pounds in the sixth grade, Jean Clark, Molly Akins, and Ruby Lathem couldn't wait until they were old enough to go to USO dances if any ever came to Bodark Springs. They all planned to marry soldiers—or maybe sailors or marines. Ellie Pearl said, "I aim to marry me a Coast Guard sailor and live in a lighthouse down at Gal VEST un."

Miss Pate, who taught fifth grade, definitely did not love the war. She had been engaged to marry Whit Baker, but his

National Guard unit got called up a month before the wedding. He was off at Fort Polk in Louisiana training with the horse cavalry when Pearl Harbor was bombed, and he was shipped to the Philippines before he ever got leave. He died on New Caledonia in 1944.

Miss Pate—she must have had a first name but nobody ever heard it—had only an "A" gasoline sticker and had to move from her family's house in Honey Grove into a rented room in Bodark Springs. Her sticker only got her four gallons a week, so she couldn't make the drive to Stonewall Jackson Elementary School five days a week. It was hard for her, but she spent the war years in a room in Mrs. Bernice Gooch's house. She never complained to the students or faculty, but she wrote her mother that Bernice Gooch was the nastiest housekeeper in Eastis County.

In early May of 1943, Mr. Vann, the school principal, announced in assembly that Virgil Junior Fotner had joined the Marine Corps.

When Tommy Earl told Grady Dell at supper that night, Grady asked, "What grade was that Fotner boy in?"

"Same as me," Tommy Earl said, "the fifth. He was in Miss Pate's room."

"The fifth? Wait a minute. You can't just join the service out of the fifth grade."

"He was seventeen in March, Miss Pate said. He didn't even have to get his folks' permission to join up."

"And he was still in the fifth grade with you little kids? He must be as dumb as his daddy."

"Who was his daddy?" Mamie asked.

Grady said, "Oh, you know old Virgil Fotner, that tie hacker that grew up somewhere up north on the Red River. Probably across the Red. Probably was a damned Okie if the truth was known. He's married to Itry."

Mamie said, "That's right. I do know them Fotners. Itry Fotner must weigh four hundred pounds. She's so fat she can't get in a car, and the only way she can go to town is sitting in the back end of a wagon with her feet hanging off. They are all dumb as oxen—and she's fat as one."

"And mean," Tommy Earl said. "I hated Virgil Junior Fotner and I'm glad he left Bodark because he used to cuff us little boys around and call us little sumbitches."

Grady got red in the face and said, "Don't you ever let nobody call you a son of a bitch. You hear me? If anybody does, you just double up your fist and hit him in the mouth."

Tommy Earl knew not to hit Virgil Junior Fotner in the mouth or anywhere else. He didn't like being slapped and called a sumbitch, but he knew what would happen if he ever hit Virgil Junior Fotner. So he said, "Yessir, I sure won't."

Virgil Junior Fotner only learned when he joined the US Marines that he was Virgil Fotner, Junior. He argued with the recruiter over the name. "My name is Virgil Junior Fotner, not Virgil Fotner, Junior."

The recruiter asked, "What is your father's name?"

"Virgil Fotner. Why?"

The sergeant entered him in the US Marine Corps enlistment as Fotner, Virgil, Jr., and that was the name on the coffin that returned him to Bodark Springs after he was killed at Guadalcanal later in the war.

Virgil Junior Fotner was not the only fifth-grade casualty in Tommy's year. Nellie Attaway left the fifth grade to get married. One day, Mr. Vann knocked on Miss Pate's door and asked her to bring Nellie out in the hall. Nellie's mother and a man were waiting just outside the door. Nellie rushed back in to get her sweater and said, "I am getting married. I really am! I am getting married today!" And she flew out the door. While Miss Pate and Mr. Vann were going to the office to get Nellie signed out, the fifth graders ran to the window just in time to see Nellie and her mother get into a 1931 Model A Ford with bright yellow wheels. Miss Pate shooed the kids back to their seats, but the hubbub went on all through geography period. Miss Pate had to threaten to whip Ellie Pearl for giggling about Nellie's "old grandfather of a husband." Somebody learned that the fifteen-year-old Nellie Attaway was marrying a forty-five-year-old man. But at least he had a 1931 Model A Ford with yellow wheels.

Not long after Virgil Junior Fotner joined up, the draft board began classifying lots of Eastis County boys 1-A, and letters from President Franklin D. Roosevelt started arriving, saying "Greetings, your friends and neighbors have selected you . . ."

Tommy Earl and the Martin brothers and Fred Hallmark all bragged about how they would get in the service someday. If only this war would last long enough.

"I can't wait till I see a Jap down the end of my rifle," J. T. said.

"Naw," Fred said, "I want to go over to Germany and kill me some of them Krauts. Hell, I'd like to get a shot at old Hitler hisself. I'd hit him right in the mustache. That silly looking sumbitch."

The war would not last long enough for Tommy and Fred and J. T. and Roy and Hal Holley to serve, but it ran on long enough to wear out a lot of mothers and fathers who had sons and daughters in the fighting. Tommy and his friends might have loved World War II, but the boys dodging bullets and being killed and wounded hated it. It lasted forever for some of those brought home in coffins or missing in action. Or buried at sea.

A few days after Pearl Harbor was bombed, the whittlers and tobacco chewers who filled the lawn chairs on the courthouse square gathered to solve the war problem. Whit Moore said, "Hell, the damn Japs won't last six weeks once we get after 'em.

You ever see that stuff they make that says 'Made in Japan' on it? A damn Jap cooking pot looks like it's made out of tinfoil."

Old man Horace Talley, a Spanish War veteran who thought he was a wit, said, "You know, they ought to call it 'Earl Harbor.'"

Whit Moore spat out a stream of tobacco juice and said, "What the hell are you talking about?"

"I said they ought to call it Earl Harbor because the Japs bombed the pee out of it. Git it?"

"You miserable old son of a bitch, I ought to slap a skillet of piss out of you."

"Why don't you just try it, you skinny bastard!"

"Boys! Stop this wrangling." It was Herman Wells, the county sheriff. "You know, don't you, that that McBrier boy and James Weller got killed when they made that sneak attack on Pearl Harbor? So just remember it is Pearl with a capital 'P,' Mr. Talley."

The high sheriff of Eastis County, who had been in the Marine Corps at Belleau Woods in World War I, turned and walked away. Nobody spoke, and soon the old men on the square drifted away. The sheriff had the lawn chairs removed the next day, and there were no whittlers on the square for the rest of the war.

Things looked dark in Bodark all through 1942. The Germans were masters of Europe, and the Japanese had taken the Philippines and chunks of Southeast Asia. Even the Italians were menacing. As soon as Grady Dell got in from his route, he read every word of the *Sherman Democrat* to get the war news. After supper, he twisted the dials of the radio to get the latest awful news of the war. He listened to H. V. Kaltenborn, Edward R. Murrow, and Gabriel Heatter, who often started his broadcast with, "There's bad news tonight." Grady kept a world map tacked up to his and Mamie's bedroom wall with blue pins for the Axis and red pins for the Allies. After his paper and his radio news, he would move the pins around on the map. As the Allies lost ground in Asia, he struggled to find Singapore and Sumatra and Hong Kong. When the war in the desert had Rommel's Africa Corps rushing westward, Grady hunted for Tunis and Casablanca.

One night, late in 1942, Grady drank more than usual and told Mamie, "Tomorrow, when I get off from work, I am heading for Sherman to try and join the army."

"Are you plumb crazy? You are fifty-two years old and fat and have had at least one heart attack and a mild stroke. They ain't about to let you get into a soldier suit. You can just forget that."

"Well, it ain't right for young fellers just starting out to go out there and die when lots of us old World War I veterans'll make better cannon fodder than boys like them two Brasher brothers who died on Corregidor or that Lawler boy who went down with the *USS Houston* somewhere in the Pacific. I've pretty much lived my life. They ought to send old men to war and let the young 'uns alone."

Nothing came of Grady's threat to join the army. But when he had drunk too much of Tubby Wallace's liquor, he still mumbled about how he needed "to go and fight the goddamn Germans that we whipped in nineteen and eighteen. It looks like you have to whip them sons of bitches every twenty-five years."

Tommy Earl and Fred and the Martin boys and Hal Holley started the sixth grade in the fall of 1944, and by then the whole idea of "Home Front" had taken hold of East Texas. Posters were up everywhere showing Hitler, Hirohito, and Mussolini as evil animals. Hitler was a snake, Mussolini a fat toad, and Hirohito a spider. Americans were warned that loose lips sank ships and that we should "Use It Up, Wear It Out, Make It Do, or Do Without." By then everybody had a ration book, and meat, tires, gasoline, shoes, coffee, and sugar were rationed. What wasn't rationed was often in short supply, and many stores ran out of such staples as butter, eggs, bread, and lard. The Office of Price Administration put ceiling prices on most goods, and posters went up saying, "KEEP THE HOME FRONT PLEDGE: Never Pay More Than Ceiling Prices. Pay Your Points in Full."

Despite the OPA and the ration points and the "meatless Tuesdays," there was a little black-market racketeering going on, even in patriotic Bodark Springs, Texas. Everybody believed that if the money was right, J. W. McCraney could slip you a couple of tires or a few gallons of gas that he claimed had evaporated.

Even smokers had a hard time of it. Tobacco companies were sending thousands of cigarettes to the fighting men, and the supply for the Home Front (always printed in capital letters) was sharply curtailed. As the American Tobacco Company said in its ads, "Lucky Strike Green Has Gone to War." For some reason that nobody in Bodark understood, the Lucky Strike package went from green to white "for the war effort."

Grady and Mamie Dell were serious smokers and had to resort to roll-your-own cigarettes. Grady bought a cigarette roller machine and pouches of Bugler tobacco. At night, he and Mamie would roll up forty or fifty smokes and put them in the Camels or Luckies packs they saved back from the few times the drugstore would let them have a package of ready-rolls.

Tommy Earl and Fred Hallmark started smoking in 1943 when Tommy got a job at Jimmy Pounds's drugstore. The store got five or six cartons of cigarettes a week, but Mr. Pounds kept them under the counter for special customers. Anyone who was not a regular was told that the store had no cigarettes. Now that Tommy Earl was making twenty cents an hour jerking soda, he could afford the fifteen cents that a pack of Phillip Morris cigarettes cost. Tommy and Fred had grown up smoking a little rabbit tobacco and some crossvine and corn silk, so it was not much of a jump to store-bought cigarettes. Fred had a job at C. C. Reed's grocery store and could sneak the occasional pack of Wings or Old Golds or Picayunes out from under the counter. Tommy's folks had no idea that he smoked because he kept his packs at Fred's house in the garage behind some feed sacks. Since both parents smoked, the smell of tobacco on Tommy Earl was hidden by the fog that Mamie and Grady kept going in the house.

When Mr. Vann, the principal, caught Tommy Earl and Fred Hallmark smoking a block off the campus, he said, "Don't you boys know that smoking will stunt your growth? Our soldiers and sailors need cigarettes out where they are fighting and dying, and here you two are smoking like chimneys. I better not catch a cigarette on my school grounds. I'll tell Chief Orr Starnes about you two juvenile delinquents."

"Nossir, nossir! We don't smoke regular. We just bummed cigarettes off that colored guy at the filling station."

"It is 'regularly,' not 'regular.' Learn about the adverb or I'll have you in my office after school."

"Yessir, 'regularly.'"

"Oh, and another thing. Are you boys working in the scrap drive and collecting paper and bacon grease for the war effort?"

"Oh, yessir, we are. Me and Fred are Home Front officers in Mrs. Lawler's sixth-grade room."

"Good. Good. And, Tommy Earl, it is 'Fred and I,' not 'me and Fred.' I may have to speak to Mrs. Lawler about your grammar."

"Yessir," they both said.

When the county noticed that Tommy Earl didn't have a work permit, he had to leave his job at the drugstore, but he still managed to find a way to smoke. He didn't need a work permit to deliver cleaning for Smith McMasters at Bodark Springs Cleaners and Laundry ("We Wash for White People Only") because McMasters paid him in cash—$2.50 a week. His friend Bert Kerlee, who was the head soda jerk at the drugstore, would usually let Tommy have a package or two a week, though his favorite Phillip Morris brand was often sold out and he had to make do with Wings or Picayunes.

The early days of the war set everybody in Eastis County to scavenging. Every grade at the Stonewall Jackson challenged every other grade in saving paper, scrap metal, tinfoil, bacon grease, aluminum toothpaste tubes, and rubber bands. They even brought in lard cans filled with bacon grease (everybody said it was supposed to be used in making explosives, but nobody knew that for sure). The teachers gave the students military ranks for the amount of stuff they brought in. First and second graders were usually corporals and sergeants, the upper grades were captains and majors. Ladell Moseley, the banker's son, was a colonel since he not only brought in the best scrap, but had the money to buy whole war bonds and not just stamps like the rest of his classmates did.

War stamps cost a quarter, and a full book of stamps would get you an $18.75 war bond redeemable in ten years for $25.00. There were higher denominations, but few in Bodark Springs ever bought the $50.00 and $100.00 war bonds. Nobody realized that inflation would wipe out the maturity of the bonds in the early 1950s.

The Depression had been hard in Eastis County, but as the war wore on, jobs opened up. Old man Horace Talley bragged about how his boy Mason was making big money. One day in McLaughlin's Feed and Seed Store, he said, "My boy Mason works over at the Arsenic."

Smith McLaughlin said, "He does what?"

"I told you, he works over at the Red River Arsenic making powder and bullets and what not to send off and kill Japs."

When Tommy heard this exchange, he wondered about how

arsenic was used in killing people. He knew it killed rats. But he didn't know about killing the enemy. It made sense. After all, arsenic was poison. As bad or worse than strychnine.

When Smith, who had turned away and tried not to laugh at old man Talley, got Tommy aside, he told him that Mason Talley worked at the Red River Arsenal over close to Texarkana. Tommy Earl liked calling it "the Arsenic" so well that he kept calling it that long after the war was over.

Wages went up all across the country when the war got well underway. Men who had chopped cotton or hoed corn or baled hay for fifty cents a day found jobs in Dallas and Fort Worth and even in Sherman making the unheard of sum of $1.00 an hour, plus time-and-a-half for overtime. If you were too old for the draft or had been declared 4-F because of flat feet or a bad back or some other ailment, you could at last find a job.

In 1940, when many men joined the army for a one-year enlistment, they were making more money than they had ever seen in civilian life. One of the songs of the day put their pay at "Twenty-one dollars a day—once a month." But $21.00 a month was not bad since the government provided three meals a day, a place to sleep (sometimes on the ground), and good army clothing. Those soldiers who joined for that one year in 1940 found themselves serving "for the duration" when the United States entered the war. Many of them didn't make it home till 1945 or 1946. And some never did. A few joined the reserves when they got discharged, and they found themselves entangled in a war in far-off Korea about five years later.

One late afternoon in 1943, Tommy Earl and Fred Hallmark got rich when a troop train got stuck on a siding off the T&P tracks in Bodark Springs. The troop train spent two hours side-tracked as it waited for a freight train with a load of tanks headed for the Eastern Seaboard. When Tommy and Fred got close to the train, soldiers started calling to them to run to a cafe and get them a hamburger and a Coca-Cola. The soldiers passed ones and fives out the train window, and Tommy and Fred ran to the Busy Bee Cafe or Powers Cafe and got hot dogs, hamburgers, and chicken salad sandwiches for the train-bound troops. Before the two hours passed, Tommy Earl had made $17.50 and Fred $14.00. They had never seen that much money at one time. They made more in that two hours than either of them had ever made for a month's work.

With all their riches, they could go to the movie every time the picture changed. They had always gone on Saturdays for the Western, the serial, and the mystery starring Boston Blackie or Charlie Chan or the Falcon. Now they could see the grade A shows like *Going My Way, Casablanca, Gaslight*, and *The Song of Bernadette*. And always the thrilling newsreels that showed the ravages of war. It was a great time for movies, and Tommy Earl fell in love with Priscilla Lane when he saw her in *Saboteur*. His love affair lasted all the way through the war, especially when she played Cary Grant's girl friend in *Arsenic and Old Lace*.

The war opened up a whole new world for Bodark Springs. The movies were filled every night, and people could afford good Philco or Atwater Kent radios so housewives of an afternoon could listen to *Stella Dallas* ("a story of mother love and sacrifice"), or *Backstage Wife*, or *Lorenzo Jones* ("Lorenzo's inventions made him a character to the town, but not to his wife Belle who loves him"). In the evenings, after the war news, whole families could listen to Jack Benny and Bob Hope and Edgar Bergen and Charlie McCarthy. Young people chilled to the mysteries of *Inner Sanctum* and *The Shadow*—("Who knows what evil lurks in the hearts of men?"). Grownups loved *One Man's Family* and *Lux Radio Theatre*, and a whole nation waited nightly for Fibber McGee to open his famous closet at 79 Wistful Vista and hear the great crashes that followed. And people took to using Molly's line, "It ain't funny, McGee" when somebody told a bad joke.

Saturday nights were given over to *Your Hit Parade* for the young and up to date and *The Grand Ole Opry* for people who had grown up listening to Jimmie Rodgers and Gene Autry and Bob Wills. The *Hit Parade* was on NBC, but the *Opry* came across on WSM in Nashville, which billed itself as "The Air Castle of the South," and good radios across the country could pick up "clear-channel" WSM as well as *The National Barn Dance* from Chicago's WLS.

Tommy Earl hated it when Grady tuned in *The Grand Ole Opry.* He couldn't stand Ernest Tubb and his Texas Troubadors or Gid Tanner and the Skillet Lickers or the banjo picker Uncle Dave Macon and his son Dorris.

Tommy Earl asked Grady, "How come Uncle Dave Macon gave his son a girl's name?"

Grady knew the answer, but Tommy Lee was sorry he had asked. Grady droned on and on about Uncle Dave from McMinnville, Tennessee. He said, finally, "Dorris Macon is spelled with two 'r's and that makes it a man's name. Now Uncle Dave, called 'the Dixie Dewdrop,' and Dorris and some others make up a group called the 'Fruit Jar Drinkers,' and they was all in a movie with Roy Acuff and George D. Hay, the one they call 'the solemn old judge.' What do you think about that? Does that answer your question?"

"I reckon." But he still thought it sounded like a girl's name.

Tommy Earl and his friends liked *Your Hit Parade* and hated—hated! hated! hated!—the *Opry.*

If Glenn Miller or Benny Goodman or Harry James or Glen Gray and the Casa Loma Orchestra didn't play a song, they quickly lost interest. The jukeboxes they liked didn't play hillbilly music. They played Bing Crosby and "Her Nibs Miss Georgia Gibbs" and Lanny Ross and bands like Sammy Kaye and the Dorsey Brothers.

One night in the summer of 1943, Tommy Earl took a bath,

rubbed a heavy dose of Three Flowers Brilliantine on his hair and announced that he was going with Fred and J. T. to "the Colonel's Corner."

Grady said, "Hold on a minute. What is this Colonel's Corner you're talking about? What do they do there that makes you put all that 'slickum' on your hair?"

"The Colonel's Corner is a dance club for teenagers sponsored by the Civitan Club, and they send you home by eleven o'clock sharp."

"You're not a teenager yet, and you got no business hug dancing with a bunch of little old shimmy-tailed girls. You probably don't even know how to dance."

"I will be a teenager before long, and I'm big for my age. Fred's already thirteen, and everybody thinks we're the same age. And I been practicing up on dancing."

"Practicing where?" Grady wanted to know.

"Over at Helen Hawkins's house. She has lots of records—Tommy Dorsey and Jimmy Dorsey and Glenn Miller and all of Bing's songs. Her momma lets her roll up the rug in the living room and show me how to jitterbug and round dance and all."

"Jitterbug? What in the world are you talking about? Jitterbug? Is that some kind of dance or what? And how old is that Hawkins girl anyway? Is she old John T. Hawkins's girl? If she is, she ought to be in high school by now."

Tommy Earl said, "She is sixteen, but I don't know Mr. Hawkins's first name. But she can dance like nobody's business, and she likes to teach me. She's not any taller than I am, and since her boyfriend went off into the air corps she don't have nobody to dance with."

Grady walked out on the porch with Tommy Earl out of Mamie's hearing and said, "Now, you are only twelve—"

"—Nearly thirteen," Tommy said.

"Yeah, well, but that Hawkins girl's way too old for you, and she has had a boyfriend who is even older. So you don't know what might happen. You could catch yourself a case of the Old Dog. So you look out, boy."

"Yessir, I will."

When Tommy walked over to Fred's house to start for the dance, he wondered what his daddy had been talking about. And when he and Fred got out on the street on the way to the Colonel's Corner, he said, "Fred, what is the Old Dog?"

"What old dog are you talking about? Do you mean Roy Martin's mongrel dog or what?"

"No. What my daddy called 'the Old Dog.' My daddy said if I keep hanging out with Helen Hawkins I might catch a case of the Old Dog."

"Damned if I know. Maybe it's like the crabs."

"The whats?"

"The crabs. It's what you get from crotch-knocking with some girl that has these little bugs 'down there,'" Fred said. "You heard about that Cosby boy, didn't you? The one that went off to that motel on the Jacksboro Highway in Fort Worth with some old gal from Oklahoma. Well, he come home with a case of the crabs and had to go in and talk to Jimmy Pounds to get something to kill them."

"What do you get to kill them crabs things?"

Fred said, "Something called Blue Ointment. Hadn't you heard that song? I heard Charlie Crosby singing it down at Roy Rogers's filling station. It goes like this:" Then to the tune of "That Old Gray Bonnet (With the Blue Ribbons on It)", Fred sang,

> Put on that old blue ointment,
> To the crab's disappointment,
> Put it on three times a day.
> Oh, it burns and it itches,
> But it kills them sons of bitches,

In that good old-fashioned way.

They laughed all the way to Colonel's Corner, but Tommy Earl didn't know any more when he got to the dance than he had when he left home. How was he supposed to get the Old Dog by dancing with Helen Hawkins?

When he danced with Helen, he was careful not to get too close to her on the slow numbers in case he caught something. He hated that. After all, Helen was fully developed up top, and he really liked to hug up to her when they danced. As they slow danced, Helen said, "I'm Getting Sentimental Over You."

Tommy nearly fainted. If Helen, at sixteen, was getting sentimental over him, she might hug up later and give him the Old Dog. He didn't know what to say. Finally, he said, "What do you mean, 'sentimental'?"

She said, "I'm Getting Sentimental Over You" is the name of that song we were dancing to. It's Tommy Dorsey's theme song."

"Oh."

Tommy kept on being in love with Priscilla Lane, but Helen Hawkins showed up in his dreams more than the famous movie star did.

When food got scarce in Bodark Springs, anybody that had any ground around their houses started following Eleanor Roosevelt's advice and making plans to grow Victory Gardens.

Charlie Stone, the window clerk at the post office, had two acres of land out behind his house, and he asked Grady how hard it would be to get it plowed up and planted in vegetables.

Grady said, "If it was me, I would get Jimmy Kelley to come and plow it up with his mule. Then you can lay it off in rows and plant whatever you want to."

Charlie asked if Jimmy Kelley was that yellow nigger who used to come through town with a mule and wagon hauling watermelons in the summer.

"Well, Charlie, I don't think I would call Jimmy Kelley a yellow nigger if I was going to ask him to work for me. Let's say 'colored.' I've known Jimmy Kelley since he was a yearling boy, and I have pretty much forgot what race he is. He has always been nice and respectful to me, and his momma used to give me pies and cakes around Christmastime. She was born a slave over in Red River County, and I have heard that her daddy was a white man. Maybe that's why Jimmy is light-skinned."

Pretty soon everybody in town starting hunting up Jimmy Kelley to break up their yards for planting. Jimmy brought his turning plow in his wagon, unhitched the mule, hooked him up to the plow's singletree and broke yard after yard. He had never made as much money in his life. He got from two to three dollars depending on the size of the yard. By late spring, Bodark Springs was like a big truck farm with potatoes and tomatoes and peas and okra and snap beans all in the ground and showing green. City dwellers who had never lived on a farm read agriculture department pamphlets and became experts in eggplants and broccoli and other strange vegetables that Eastis County natives had never heard of.

As the war wore on, government bureaus proliferated. There was the Office of War Information, the dreaded Selected Service System, the War Production Board, the Office of Defense Transportation ("Is This Trip Really Necessary?"), and the Office of Civil Defense. These were only a few of the boards people got to calling by initials—WPB, OPA, ODT, and on and on. Civil defense came late to Bodark Springs. About halfway through the war, Mayor Barge McCall announced in the local paper that air raid wardens were needed immediately.

The mayor called in "Foots" Waller and asked him to be the head warden. Harry Waller was Bodark Springs's most famous citizen. A star baseball player, he had tried out with the St. Louis Cardinals in 1937 and was playing for the Cardinals' Triple A Columbus Redbirds in the American Association when war was declared. He became a permanent member of the St. Louis Cardinals when so many ballplayers were called into the service. Because he had the flattest—and biggest—feet in the county, people started calling him "Big Foot" Waller. As time passed, he became, for the folks in Eastis County and in newspapers all over the country, simply "Foots." When he was classified 4-F by the Selective Service System, the doctor who examined his feet said, "I never saw anything that big that didn't have guts in it."

Since his size sixteen flat feet kept him out of the army, he had a chance to join the stellar Cardinal pitching staff of Mort Cooper and Harry "the Cat" Breecheen, an old boy from across the Red in Broken Bow, Oklahoma. Nobody in Bodark ever referred to him as Harry Waller or just plain Harry; he was always Foots, even to the kids who hung around him at the hardware store in the off season.

Mayor McCall caught Foots coming out of his father-in-law's hardware store one November morning and said, "I think I have a job that you are perfect for, Foots."

"A job? I have a job here in the hardware store in the winter, and when baseball season starts, I have a real job pitching for the Cardinals. I don't reckon I need another one, Mayor."

McCall said, "This ain't a paying job, Foots. This is for the war effort. And since it is winter and you ain't playing ball, I need you to head up the civil defense team for Bodark Springs. I want you to serve as chief air raid warden."

Foots said, "Shoot, Mayor, I don't know nothing about civilian defense, or whatever you call it. What's an air raid warden? Don't tell me we are gonna have air raids like they did in England?"

"No, no, I doubt that we will have air raids here in Bodark, but Franklin D. Roosevelt says we have to have blackouts and wardens and get ready just in case. All you would have to do is to sit down in the city hall and stay on the phone during the blackouts and see that everybody in Bodark has turned the lights out. You'll have a messenger to send out to the wardens on the street, to, to, well, I don't know, send them messages. Will you do it? You are the best-known man in town. Everybody respects you."

Foots agreed to serve until spring training started, and he picked Tommy Earl Dell as his messenger since Foots and his wife Dot lived out on Grady's route and liked the postman. Besides, Tommy Earl was always pestering Foots to teach him how to throw a curve and a drop.

He told Dot, "That boy won't never learn how to throw a curveball, but he might make a good messenger. He looks fast."

Tommy Earl was equipped with a white helmet that must have weighed ten pounds. On the front of the helmet in a triangle was a lightning bolt that signified the speed of the messenger. The wardens had similar white helmets, but theirs had a CD in the triangle where Tommy's lightning bolt was.

Grady Dell was one of the wardens, but he questioned the utility of air raid wardens so far from the coasts. He told Homer Brantley that this whole business was foolishness. He said, "Where do they think these bombers are gonna come from? Are they gonna fly way over here from Germany? Hell, I have been to Germany, and it took me five days to get from New Jersey to Liverpool on a boat back in nineteen and eighteen. And when you get to Liverpool, England, you ain't much more than halfway there."

Homer said, "What is there to bomb in Bodark Springs anyway?"

Grady said, "Nothing. But Foots said at our first meeting that these planes would be headed to that bomber plant in Fort Worth and that if Bodark was all lit up, they could plot a course right over Dallas and on to Fort Worth."

"Bullshit. How far would these planes have to travel did you say? Five or six thousand miles? And then what would they do? Turn around and fly back? You people are wasting your time if you ask me."

"Well, Homer, they didn't ask you. Or me either. But since I am a veteran and all, I am gonna see that people turn out the lights when we have a blackout. My boy Tommy Earl has a pretty important job his own self. He is Foots Waller's messenger."

On the night of the big blackout—the only blackout Bodark Springs ever had—Foots and Tommy Earl Dell sat in the little two-room city hall as the fire siren went off announcing the start of the air raid drill. Before long, Mayor McCall rang up Foots and said, "There is a light showing over at Gladys Lundy's apartment up over the dry cleaners. Get the warden over there to make her draw her blackout curtain or turn out the light."

It was a dark night with the new moon barely over the horizon, but Tommy Earl, decked out in his white helmet and CD armband, rushed out in the darkness and tried to find Ned Rew, the warden in that part of downtown. He rushed up and said to the warden, "Foots says have Gladys Lundy douse that light."

Ned was nearly drunk, and he said to Tommy, "You go tell her to cut out the light if Foots wants it out. I'm too old to walk up them steps to her place just to say something silly."

Tommy Earl ran up the steps, banged on the door, and screamed, "Turn out that light! Don't you know there's a war on?"

Gladys was half drunk herself and hollered back, "Get away from my door, you little runt. I got company in here. Tell Foots and Ned Rew I said, 'Go to hell.'"

It was that way all over Bodark Springs that night. Nobody paid much attention to the blackout. All the street lights were out, and the stores turned off their lights. But there were lots of slants of light peeping out from curtains as people sat listening to *Amos 'n' Andy* on the radio. The Kingfish was saying, "Holy mackerel, Andy!" when the siren went off ending the blackout. That ended the whole civil defense action in Bodark Springs, and things went back to normal as the war turned in the Allies' favor in 1943 and 1944.

Germany surrendered in 1945. Roosevelt died that same year. And a few of the soldiers and sailors began drifting back to Eastis County as they were invalided out of the services. Some limped home on canes, one or two had lost limbs, and one old boy from up the county spent the rest of his life in a wheelchair. Many of them looked shocked and depressed.

Tommy Earl was flipping hamburgers at a little cafe that Willie Speidel opened up over on Railroad Avenue in the summer of 1945. Mrs. Willie Speidel couldn't hope to compete with Bear Higgins at the Busy Bee Cafe or with Powers Cafe up by the Greyhound bus stop, but she was far enough on the wrong side of the tracks to do a little business.

Tommy Earl was fixing two hamburgers "all the way" for Lonnie Maubrey to take home when Hal Holley rushed in the front door and said, "They dropped a bum no bigger than a baseball on them Japs!"

Willie said, "They done what? What do you mean bum?"

Hal said, "They called it a atom bum, and it tore up a whole city. Mr. C .C. Reed over at the grocery store says the war with Japan won't last now. That's all I know. I have to run home and tell Momma that Russell oughta be coming home soon."

Before it was all over, more than thirty boys and three girls from Eastis County died in that war. Otis Lawson's boy won the Medal of Honor, and Helen Hawkins, who joined the WAFs, died in a plane crash in West Texas. A girl nobody knew who came from folks up on the Red River died in England from a Buzz Bomb just before the war was over in Europe.

The worst casualty on the Home Front came when Lucille Brooks drank Drano and killed herself when she learned that Hollis Marshall was bringing home a British war bride. Lucille called Myrt Marshall, Hollis's sister, who was Bodark's night telephone operator, and said, "Myrt, I am going to kill myself. I am going to do it right now, and I want you to hear me die." She drank the Drano and was trying to tell Myrt something when the lye burned out her vocal chords and Myrt heard her last strangles.

About the Author

Photo by Ruth McAdams, 2012

James Ward Lee is emeritus professor and former chair of the English department at the University of North Texas. He is past president and now a fellow of the Texas Folklore Society. He is author of over a hundred articles, stories, and reviews and is author or editor of ten books. He is founding director of UNT Press and the Center for Texas Studies at UNT. Lee was founding editor of the journals *Studies in the Novel*, *American Literary Review*, and *New Texas*. His most recent books are *Adventures with a Texas Humanist*, *Texas Country Singers* (with Phil Fry), and *Literary Fort Worth* (coedited with Judy Alter). James Lee was inducted into the Texas Institute of Letters in 1974 and became a member of the Texas Literary Hall of Fame in 2010. He lives in Fort Worth.